Dezi Golden

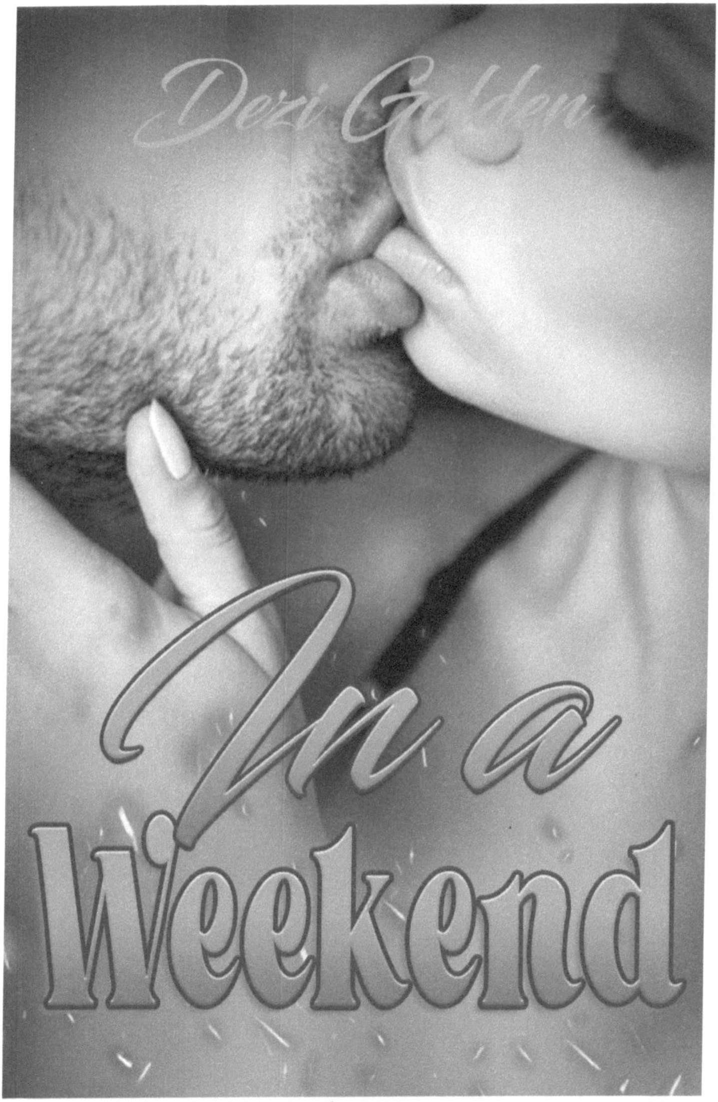

In a Weekend

IN A WEEKEND

DEZI GOLDEN

To those who believe in the bliss...

CHAPTER 1

STAY OR GO

"What the fuck."

Inhaling long she stretches her arms up then out letting them fall listlessly onto her stomach. Her eyes flutter open, despite morning sun causing confusion. Enya's mouth is dry, her legs cold. She looks down at her body splayed out in the driver's seat and feels the failure again. She never did make it to the beach house. The storm was relentless. She decides a jeep isn't the easiest vehicle to maneuver when frustrated, confused, and above all mentally exhausted. She runs her hand down her face trying to wake, convinced she'll never buy a vehicle so uncomfortable again. Then again, a Jeep really wasn't her first choice... actually she remembers it wasn't her choice at all.

She's always been the sensible one. Her idiot spouse brought it home to surprise her instead of allowing her the free will to choose her own transportation. She'd always hated his attention-seeking gifting and his constant financial control.

Reaching forward for the steering wheel she pulls her aching body upright and pushes the seat buttons until she finds the one that moves the back of the seat up to meet her tired spine. The sky is blue, cloudless, and absolutely gorgeous. Looking left she sees the ocean. It's acting as if it's reserved and calm, like last night's storm never happened. She huffs a laugh and shakes her head. The beach is beautiful and she decides to push yesterday behind her. Pushing the window button she puts it down to inhale the sea air. As expected it smells magnificent! She lets out an exasperated sigh and runs her fingers through her long red locks.

Seagulls cry in the distance. There's a hint of humidity in the air but she doesn't care. She decides today is already the best day ever compared to finding Trent in bed yesterday with another unsuspecting bimbo. She actually feels sorry for the girl. She has no clue whats coming and Enya knows she shouldn't even care as they've been estranged for over a year. She regrets going back to the house for the mail and actually thought it was safe to go during the day when he was supposed to be at work. *Yeah, why the hell was he not at work?*

Enya squeezes the thought away and turns the engine on. She decides she will find this elusive beach house if it's the last damn thing she does. *What could go wrong...*

With the windows cracked just enough, she can hear the crunch of her tires along the hidden driveway smeared with sand and broken shells. The house is much larger than Jenna lead on and is not two but three stories up on stilts! It's lovely.

As she comes closer and over a small hill she can see a work truck, materials and equipment strewn everywhere, a shutter hanging from one of the top floor windows, and what appears to be repairs happening! *What the fuck.*

Immediately annoyed she stops, mid-driveway, holding her foot on the break. Enya tries to reconcile if she should just throw the towel in and turn around back to Jenna and Harry's. She doesn't want to spend another weekend locked in their spare bedroom writing. She feels like she's losing her creativity. Her brain can't think straight these days. Seeing chaos and a mess, at an already strange house, makes her feel she should just give up. Throw the towel in and go back. *But to what En?*

The music reaches her. The volume isn't too loud but a bit more than she'd like at nine o'clock in the morning. She recognizes the CCR song, and thinks at least the workers have good taste in music.

Squinting she tries to figure out where she's supposed to park with so much shit all over the driveway. Off to the right she sees what appears to be a parking spot under the actual house. She had noticed there are no garages with the beach houses, instead homeowners seem to protect their vehicles by parking under the stilted homes. Not quite sure if she should stay, her eyes evert to movement. Suddenly he appears. He moves gracefully from around the side of the house towards his truck. He takes notice of her, stopped in the distance of the driveway. He nods and bends into his front seat for his water. Enya's mind screams "turn around and go girl!", but her heart makes her foot come off the brake rolling the car forward towards the most beautiful man she's ever seen.

2

LUCKY

"If you can, you might want to give it a chance..."

Ayson Ford tilts his head back to drink water. His long sun bleached hair falls from his shoulders and hangs long down his back. He throws the empty plastic bottle on the front seat and takes the hair tie from his wrist to tame his wild frock. His mother would have kissed him for his grooming. She always loved when he grew his hair long, he always loved how free she encouraged him to be. He turns again and sees the Jeep coming towards the house wondering if he should put a shirt on.

When the sun glare moves from the windshield he sees her. Wild red hair falling around her face, eyes frowning. Instead of a shirt he opts for more wood from the back of the truck. He keeps his face pleasant as she seems stressed and lost. Pulling a long plank from the bed of the truck he hoists it up onto his shoulder and walks around the truck back to the front of the house facing the ocean.

Enya parks under the house in the last space far from him and his mess. As large of a human as he is, she lost sight of him after he rounded the side of the house with the lumber. She slams the door and pulls her luggage on it's wheels but they don't want to roll in sand and weeds. She exhales retracting the long handle back and instead hoists the bag by its small handle trying to keep her purse on her shoulder. She follows in the direction of where the muscularly tattooed man-bun surfer looking guy went, hoping he can direct her to an entry door to the house. The breeze blows against her flip flopped toes and feels incredible but she's still not convinced she's staying. Jenna never mentioned repairs or construction being done on the house. She can't imagine spending her short three-day weekend listening to electric saws and nail guns. Also the thought of strange men working on the house way out in the middle of nowhere-island while she's there doesn't feel so safe. She really just wants to be alone.

Craning her head she tries to assess how many instruction workers are responsible for such a mess. She heaves her bag up and over pieces of lumber and materials, trying to navigate her way around the enormous house which seems to be getting bigger in size as she attempts to walk to the front.

"May I help you with that?"

Enya jumps and turns towards the melodious deep voice. Her eyes focus first on the emerald green of his eyes and then the bronzy tan of his skin. His mouth turns up slightly at the edges attempting a smile. Annoyed, she realizes she must have looked ridiculous snooping about and then jumping almost out of her skin.

"Thank you, I've got it."

"Okay?" He looks her up and down. She's obviously older than he, a bit shorter with long legs peeking gorgeously out of a very wrinkled romper she may have slept in. He thinks she's probably the most beautiful woman he's seen since moving to South Carolina years back.

"Uh-"

Her voice stops him from walking away, he places his hands on his hips, listening. His face strains from the brightness of the sun, sweat dripping down his temples. He waits for her to speak.

Enya looks around confused, "Are you here alone?"

"Are you looking to murder me?" He laughs thinking the question odd.

She frowns slightly, "What?"

"You look as if you're sizing up the place...and um-" His face is kind but his sense of humor not so much.

"I was wondering if you've made this mess all by yourself or if there are more of you is all."

He realizes she's a little high strung. She hasn't introduced herself yet and by the looks of the *one* suitcase she's solo-rented the Logan's house for the weekend. Of course she wasn't told prior about the storm damage to the front porch and upstairs shutters, because it just happened overnight. He finds her amusing and her voice mesmerizing despite her displeasure at his "mess".

"Oh, it's just me. I'm repairing a few things for The Logan's. Just the front porch there and a few shutters up on the top level. I should be out of your way with my *mess* by late afternoon ma'am."

She softens realizing she may have offended him.

"Oh, oh I see. Yes, I drove in through that storm."

"It would seem so."

She watches his eyes. He looks her up and down, then settles on her eyes.

"Ayson Ford. I'm doing the carpentry." Ayson steps forward with his hand extended.

Almost stepping back Enya stops herself and finds his hand with hers. She shakes strongly, not weak and flimsy as most women do. His firm grasp send surges through her body she can't quite understand. She likes it. His skin soft and gorgeous on the outside, a few calluses and rough patches on his inside palm. As he stepped close she caught his scent. Faded cologne, sweat, and fresh linen mixed with a little bit of lumber dust. She remembers her father's garage suddenly. She misses him. Something burns within her core. She's surprised at how her body reacts to him. Shrugging it off to his charming good looks she lifts her eyes to his man-bun and the hair thats fallen out of it waving in the breeze. She's not usually into the "man-bun" thing but he's changing her mind.

"Enya Ryan. Ayson?"

"Yep. Ayson…like Jason."

"Your mom think you were *lucky*?"

He smiles, impressed that she knows the meaning of his name, "That she did."

"Hmmm."

"Survived a car accident. Premature by a month."

Enya nods admiring his large six-foot-five frame and overly built chest. She always thinks it odd when massive humans say they were once premature.

"The steps aren't built at the moment so I'll help you? If I could, I'd like to bring your suitcase up the ladder so you don't have to."

"Oh, Oh I see." She realizes why he wants to help her. The storm removed the porch steps and he's not even halfway through building the new set. "Well, in that case then."

Ayson smiles and picks up her suitcase. Leading the way, he guides her through the sandy path to the front of the house. She steps into the footprints he leaves with his work-boots trying not to get too much sand in her flip flops. It doesn't work very well. Looking forward she sees his sculpted v-shaped back and broad shoulders. He's covered them in impressive black shaded tattoos which she admits looks fucking hot glistening with his sweat. His muscle moves fluidly beneath his tight skin. She can't help but wonder if his legs are just as dark beneath the snug Levi's jeans that hug every damn gifted area he's got. *Gawd and baby Jezus...*

He stops at a ladder along the opposite side of the porch and walks up three rungs then heaves the suitcase up onto the porch. Enya expects that he'll climb the rest of the way up and help her but he jumps down instead and offers a hand to help her now climb the rungs. A bit unprepared she cautiously tries to hoist herself using both hands along side the ladder. The angle is just so that she's aware her tush is approaching his face. She tries to hurry knowing he can see a million wrinkles in the fabric of her romper. Admittedly, she's not feeling her confidence. The sand on the bottom of her shoe slides off a rung abruptly and she starts to fall!

"Uh!!"

Ayson catches her by the waist with one hand but the other end ups palm open, holding her ass almost in her crack. Not exactly what he was going for. Her purse swings around and clocks him right in the head but he holds her from falling all the same. Her shin bangs against the step causing her to yelp.

"Oh wow, uh are you all right?"

She raises up quickly as his hand feels warm and way too nice near her gluteal cleft.

"Yes, I'm so sorry. I didn't securely grasp my foot on the step."

Ayson smiles thinking of how, even though not intended, he got a very good *grasp*.

"It's an old ladder. Here, let's take a look at that shin." He bounds up the rungs like nothing and has her face him on the porch. Bending down he can see the blood pooling underneath the wound and blood beginning to exit a small gash.

"It's not that bad. It'll bruise is all."

"True, it'll bruise all right, but let's get it so it doesn't grow into one of those big nasty yellow-purple ones or infect from that cut. Here, the kitchen is right this way." Ayson touches her elbow to guide her.

Enya realizes he's kinder than she originally thought and follows him as his tender energy is growing on her. She feels silly for what just transpired but instead of making jokes or making fun of her as her husband would, he offers to help. She likes that he's mature and follows him into what appears to be a extraordinarily Feng Shui styled house! The colors and furniture all seem to be so calming. She feels peace, and wonders if it's the home or *his* actual energy.

The kitchen is contemporary and modern with beautiful shades of white and chocolate browns. She watches him move around it as if he knows where everything is. She wonders if he built the house since he's currently building the porch on the outside. He knows right where the first aid kit is in the pantry and gets some ice from the freezer then places it in a ziplock.

"Ms. Ryan, have a seat for a second. If we ice this right away you won't feel much of it in the morning. You don't want to be limping through your entire weekend."

She huffs agreeing and takes a seat at the counter bar stool. *Only if the limping was from a wild night with you Mr. Ford.*

She smiles at her inappropriate and unexpected thought. Her purse falls to the floor with a thud. She smirks but pays it no mind. Ayson comes around placing his items on the counter and methodically preparing them. He lowers his arm to find her leg and brings it up to rest on the opposite bar chair. Her eyes affix to the shaded tattoos on his forearms both inside and out. He has exquisite taste in body art and what appears to be an intense story. Quickly he cleans and bandages her cut so he can place the cold gel pack on it. His hands work confidently and fast.

"Okay, keep that elevated for twenty minutes with the cold compress, then take it off for twenty. After about three times you'll be good to go. Might want to ice it one or two more times tonight before bed if you can. Your body will do the rest."

He begins to clean up the bandages and wipe down the counter. She didn't expect him to be so tidy by the mess left in the driveway.

"Thank you. That was so quick. The throbbing has ceased."

"Twelve years riding the ambulance has rubbed off." He chuckles.

Enya's eyebrows raise slightly. He just became ten times sexier in her eyes.

"Oh right. So carpentry isn't your day job?"

"No, just a hobby. I'm doing that for free since the Logans refused to charge me a proper rent. They're the nicest landlords. I've replaced this kitchen and most the rooms so far and they still try to pay for everything. I tell them that's not how things work." Ayson smiles sweetly.

"Rent?"

"Yes, I live on the third floor." He juts a thumb up towards the ceiling. Enya looks up, Jenna did not mention anything about him or the Logans. She's not so sure she wants to stay now.

"Oh, I didn't know."

"Don't worry. I won't be in your hair this weekend."

"No, I uh-"

"You won't hear me at all. In fact, I'm thinking of sleeping on the beach tonight now that the storm has passed."

Enya looks up at him, "You sleep on the beach?"

"Every chance I get or the boat. I enjoy a fire…and well, water. On the weekends mostly. I have a rather large tent, one of those real quick-assembly ones. I'll give you your space here since it doesn't look as if you were aware of how the rental works?" He searches her face but then washes his hands and begins making his way towards the door.

"I just wasn't aware of what sort of rental it was. My sister, uh Jenna, she didn't quite explain it all… then again, I probably just wasn't listening…"

He turns, "It's a beautiful place Ms. Ryan. If you can, you might want to give it a chance…but if you're not feeling comfortable, the Conve Inn is down the road three more miles. They may have vacancy."

She tilts her head, "Enya please. How'd you know I was thinking about going to an inn?"

He smiles and looks deep into her eyes making her feel a bit exposed, "I know a lot about healing when I see it. Wether you do it here at the Logans or down a ways at the inn, given the chance, this place will change everything...*Enya*." He likes the way her name sounds.

Enya straightens her back unsure of how to feel about his unsolicited advice or the fact that his leaving the room makes her yearn for him in ways she shouldn't. Ayson holds his hand up waving goodbye and opens the sliding glass door.

Once on the porch he bends picking up her luggage bag and brings it to the inside of the door giving one last look towards her.

Walking away he jumps down avoiding the ladder and shakes his head smiling. He reaches down adjusting his crotch and shifting his jeans realizing touching and bandaging Enya's long tan leg caused some unexpected reactions below his waist. He gets back into his porch project trying to erase the vision of her long red hair and those deep golden brown eyes looking up at him. He can tell she's wounded deeply and the kind of healing he would offer may not be what she's looking for.

3

HIXON

"Just let tonight be a relaxing experience."

Enya finishes putting her clothes in the drawer. There's only enough for the few days so it didn't take long. She does want to stay.

Opening the closet, she rolls her bag into it and thinks how a very large human could fit in there. She wonders if Ayson built that as well. The door mirror reflects her dreadful appearance! Her mascara has run under her eyes from sleeping in the jeep and her outfit is now frightfully wrinkled. She leans in and wipes away the excess makeup embarrassed at how she must have looked to Mr. Gorgeous Paramedic who lives on the third floor. She stops, looking deep into her reflection.

When did you get this way En?

Sighing apologetically to herself she realizes her cheating, bastard of a husband has done a number on her self-esteem. *Ugh!* She turns around opening the drawer and grabs her bikini. Stripping down out of the romper she kicks it at the closet watching it hit the mirror and slide down to the floor. She's so disappointed in herself for believing in a man who was nothing but disloyal. She's pissed at all the times she could have gone after happiness, gone for what met her needs, but instead she worried about how he'd feel! How going after what was best for her might make him feel less loved.

Fuck him!

She steps into the holes of the bikini bottoms pulling them up and feeling like they're just a smidge bigger then last time. She puts on the top and luckily can tie it tighter around the neck and back.

So you've lost some inches En, big deal.

She realizes she's even sacrificed her body for the undeserving prick. She's gone so long without intimacy because of a ring he had no honor for. She feels so done with being loyal to someone who can NEVER be.

Erasing the defeating thoughts she wraps a sarong around her waist and grabs her beach bag, a towel, and some lotion. Her body aches from sleeping in the car overnight so she decides a swim and some sunbathing will kick off her weekend nicely. Impressively her shin hardly hurts at all.

Ayson has completed quite a few more steps on the porch repair but realizes he's having trouble concentrating now that Enya is down in the ocean with a bathing suit on a bit too big for her sexy frame. The waves are beating her up and she's spending more time fixing her clothing than relaxing. He feels bad for her. She's probably come to Hixon to get away from whatever it is people are running from when they venture out this far on the island. He remembers not too long ago being similar. He only hopes she can get away from whatever she's running from in three short days.

He puts his pencil behind his ear and brings another board from the truck. Checking on her again he winces seeing a huge wave smack into her sideways sending her stumbling on that bruised shin. The water is relentless and down goes her bikini bottoms to her knees. His mouth drops and the pencil falls. He has no idea how to unsee how incredibly beautiful she is! She spins around trying to run from a second wave while desperately pulling her bottoms up. His groin hitches as he sees the curtains definitely match the drapes in a gorgeous golden shade of red! He quickly looks away so she doesn't have to feel even more embarrassed then she already is. Mortification and shock present on her face but he pretends he's busy only glancing every so many seconds while still working. Part of him wants to go help her, the other part of him wants to hold her in his arms until she begs him to make the day better.

Enya finally gives up on the ocean and makes her way to her towel. He sees she's finally putting lotion on and lying down to tan. She has a gorgeous glow to her skin already which surprises him since gingers usually burn. She's incredibly beautiful but doesn't seem to be the type to notice it. He thinks some man out there has done a number on her and whoever he is should be ashamed of himself. She needs to be loved and loved well.

An hour and a half later he's almost done his project but knows a lunch break is in order to keep going. He looks to see how she's doing. She's rolled over and appears to have fallen asleep on her tummy.

He decides she might need some food too. He doesn't want to bother her…but he also can't seem to want to be away from her either.

"Hey there."

Ayson stands far enough away to be heard and yet not startle her. She doesn't answer.

Enya inhales deep, snoring slightly, her face to one side.

"Hey?"

Nothing.

"Enya? Hungry?"

Her eye opens as she realizes there's a voice. Focusing in on the large figure standing five feet away, she jolts up forgetting she took off her top. Her breasts bounce up and Ayson turns away holding two beers and avocado sandwiches.

"Whu-" Enya looks around then down at her breasts covering them with a hand while reaching for her top with the other. She looks over and sees he's turned his back. *Oh thank ya!*

With his mouth speaking in the opposite direction he speaks cordially, "Hey, it's just me. I thought you might be hungry? I'm on a lunch break from porch-building hell."

"Oh…uh." Enya ties her bikini top hurriedly and turns over.

"Is it safe?" He turns with eyes closed as she finishes with her sarong.

"Uh, yeah…I mean yes."

He walks towards her, his smile inviting. He holds out a beer hoping she's that kind of woman. She reaches for it *and* the sandwich impressing him even more.

"May I sit or are you needing space?"

"No, uh here." She moves over so he can share her large towel-blanket. Groggy, but not at all upset that he's found her. Oddly, his energy makes her feel much safer than when alone.

"I hope I'm not disturbing your peace. I was just wondering how your leg feels?"

"Pretty good. Better than expected. I thought I'd swim and then change the bandage when I got back to the kitchen."

"Nice."

"Thank you again. I appreciate your expert care."

"My pleasure. I usually sit down here for lunch so it was nice to see you were already here. Thought the sun might have made you hungry."

She smirks, "I am starving. Haven't eaten much lately."

"Well, let's put an end to your food strike. Let me know what you think." He takes a large bite and looks out to the sea.

She does the same. "Oh myyyyyy."

"Pretty good no?"

"Very."

She admires his effort. He has a slight smile and she knows, "You saw everything didn't you?"

He smiles looking out at the ocean, "Not everything. Just that you were struggling."

"Ugh, what is it about this day..." Enya takes another bite trying to avoid self-pity.

He swigs a sip of beer, smiling wider. He's had days like this.

"It takes about a day to *start* really relaxing here. Give it a few more hours."

He reaches to bump her knee with his wrist wanting to ease her so she'll feel better. Touch is his first love language.

Enya enjoys his gesture and smiles.

"I'm trying."

"That's all you need to do. How's the food?"

"Amazing actually. I've never thought about coupling avocado with Yuengling but I think you're onto something here."

"Ah you'd be amazed at what I've coupled with beer and passed off as a meal."

"I don't doubt that." She laughs realizing he's the one relaxing her. She's genuinely enjoying his company. He's got a kind nature and seems to pay attention naturally. She looks at him and then away hoping he hasn't seen *all* of her. She's can't help but wonder what *he* looks like. He's barefoot now and by the looks of his long, flawless feet, he's probably as breathtaking with his clothes off as he is with them on.

"So where you from?"

"Oh uh, Jenningstown, south of Newton."

Ayson nods, "I'm familiar. I worked in Newton for a year before deciding on the beach life."

"Oh very cool. Carpentry or Paramedic?"

"Paramedic. It was sort of a stepping stone town. How are you liking Hixon?"

Enya smiles while chewing, "Well aside of the storm that put me to bed in my car, the foot-slip going *up* a ladder, and losing my uh…balance in the ocean?"

Ayson laughs out loud seeing her facial expressions with the tellings of all her adventure so far. She cracks up too at his amusement. They laugh together.

She continues, "I guess Hixon is growing on me." She giggles again.

He averts his eyes back to the waves, realizing how badly he wants to kiss her and make everything go away.

"Wow, I didn't realize you'd been through so much."

"Oh that's nothing compared to finding my husband in bed with yet another unsuspecting victim two days ago." She huffs, trying to shrug it off. "We've been separated for so long, I don't know why I'm even shocked. I think I'm more annoyed I had to go back to the house for paperwork and he *should* have been at work in the middle of the day…"

Ayson's eyebrows furrow. He turns to her and stops chewing, "Oh wow Enya…I'm uh, I'm really sorry to hear that."

She smiles, "Yeah, well what are ya gonna do? Now you know why I'm all the way out here on Hixon Island. Thank you Jenna."

"Well, I can understand. Again, I'm sorry you're going through what you're going through. No one deserves such betrayal…err to even have to see it. I think Jenna was onto something, helping you get away. I'm certainly glad she picked the Logan's house."

Enya's smile fades, "Thank you. I really appreciate you saying that."

They both drink more and finish eating. He now understands why such a beautiful creature wandered out in the middle of their island *alone*. She realizes he's way more charming than she thought and just sitting close to him makes her body react in ways she's never allowed with a stranger before.

"Hey, what do you say to some dinner here tonight on the beach? I don't know if you have plans. I'm having a few friends come by to play guitar and barbecue for a while. It could help keep your mind off of the man who doesn't deserve you?"

He smiles sweetly down at her and she knows she wants to say yes.

"Oh, I don't know. I don't know if I'd be much fun. I should probably-"

"I insist! It's a great time and I'd love if you would join us." He sees she's considering it. "Even if just for a little while. *Come on.* You can't come to Hixon and not party on the beach Enya."

Hearing her name spoken from his smooth sexy voice makes her warm in places within, "Well…I guess I could hang out for a bit. What can I bring?"

He's elated to hear she'll join them, "Just yourself, maybe a blanket to sit on in case you get cold. I've got everything we need in the kitchen and plenty to drink. No need to get back in that car you had to sleep in and go to town. Just let tonight be a relaxing experience. I think you'll like the way we live out here."

Although suave with his cool demeanor she can see he's happy she'll go. It feels nice to see a man excited for her company.

"Okay. I think I can do that."

4

SMITTEN

"Those two are done my love."

She looks out at the setting sun through her bedroom window. Ayson is preparing his very large beach tent near what looks like an established and well-used bonfire circle. He's freshly showered, his hair wet laying long against his Hawaiian type shirt open just enough in the front to make her quivery between her legs. Enya shocks herself at how much she admires looking at him only meeting him in the morning. He crouches down to light the bonfire exposing his low back just before his bathing suit. His skin is dark! The same tan shade as the rest of him. She chews on the tip of her finger staring, realizing he's all the same skin color even down near his plump, muscular tush. This means, he must sunbath somewhere in the nude. He's a good-looking man. She wonders how he'd feel against her skin.

Brushing her hair leaving it to lay long down her back, she ponders why she'd been so loyal to a man who could never be loyal back, when there are men like Ayson in the world. She huffs at the thought of her dedicated, good-wife image ready to put it in the past. *It's been two years Enya! Just divorce the bastard already.*

She grabs a hoodie to put over her strappy summer dress in case she gets cold and rolls up a blanket under her arm. Since Ayson mentioned no food was needed she instead grabs the small canister of weed she's brought and her tiny pipe to share. Just in case anyone wants to relax naturally. And for those who don't, she grabs a bottle of wine from her bag.

Walking in flip flops in sand is tiring. She passes right by them and down the new porch steps barefoot. Ayson seems a perfectionist and created the most detailed steps she's ever seen in just one day. She see's the paint off to the side and makes a mental note to offer him help. He's been so caring and thoughtful towards her, she wants to return in kind.

By the time she makes it out to the fire everyone is arriving. Ayson's friends appear healthy and sun-kissed just like him. He greets her, placing a hand on her low back introduces her to his friends one by one. He's very considerate and helps her feel comfortable. It's a beautiful contrast to how her husband disrespected her around his few friends, never acknowledging her or even including her in conversation.

She meets Allison who owns a local coffee shop and is married to Juan, a cop. Greg and Don are a couple both working for the township and part-time as EMTs. River is an older hippie woman who seems to be head-over-heels in love with Frank, a fireman. Ayson doesn't seem to have a sweetheart but she can't be sure by the way three of the other ladies act around him. They are touchy, but he doesn't seem to reciprocate.

Ayson looks up from barbecuing shish-kabobs and catches her staring at him. He smiles despite teasing River. It makes her feel they've shared a moment. She averts her eyes to the group and admires how well liked he is by his friends. They seem to regard him highly and tell neat tales of him making emergency services comical.

His hair is longer than she thought and hangs down in his face so he keeps running his fingers through it. The natural blondish and chocolate brown highlights from the sun compliment his tan skin and glisten in the golden light of the horizon. She exhales thinking of how magnificent he is. One of those larger-than-life types that doesn't really know it.

Enya notices he takes a seat near her. She likes it. Three much younger women walk up to their group. Now she's not so sure if he's single. He hadn't mentioned anything.

"Hey ladies, how goes it?" Ayson points to the cooler and food for them to help themselves. He moves closer to Enya leaving enough room for them to sit on his other side.

A dark haired, green-eyed beauty runs to him first, her arms extended. Enya can't deny she feels disappointment as the girl hugs him from behind, he doesn't get up but pats her arm instead. The twenty-something kisses his hair before walking over to get food.

"Hey Ays. I haven't seen you all week. Where ya been? We missed you on shift?"

Ayson tries to finish chewing before answering, "Been taking a little time off hanging here at the house. You know, some r-n-r."

Enya smiles watching his interaction, the girls notice her and look down at her sitting crossed legged on the blanket. Ayson waves his hand, "Mara, Jeanie, and Skyler this is Enya Ryan. She's staying here at the Logan's, and I was lucky enough to convince her to join our Friday night sesh-"

The girls all greet her with a wave as they smile and collect food. Ayson leans towards her and explains that all three are new interns to his EMT squad. Enya sighs silently, relieved the women are his employees. She's shocked at how much she cares so suddenly.

The night carries on fluidly. Enya finds herself very comfortable and relaxed compared to how the day started. Her cheeks begin to ache from smiling and laughing at some of their stories. Between their comical tales they sing and play guitar displaying admirable talents. Every one of them seems to have a special talent. Enya joins in by singing and realizes she is quite talented herself.

The younger girls end up leaving first despite being the last to show. They were heading off to another party. The others say goodnight soon after and Enya finds herself sitting alone around the fire with River while Frank and Ayson walk back to the house to use the bathroom and get dessert.

"Enya, what brings you out to Hixon this weekend?" River crawls around to sit next to her in Ayson's seat.

"Oh you know River, I guess I just needed a weekend away from regular life. My sister mentioned the Logan's house and insisted I spend the long weekend basking in the sun." Enya smiles.

River searches her eyes seeing pain deep within the light brown color. She caresses a strand of hair away from Enya's face. She's like the mother she never knew, "So you just met Ayson?"

"What? Uh, oh yes, this morning." She looks to the fire, "This is my first big beach gathering actually."

"Oh, this wasn't a big one. If more knew about it it'd be a full on massive party. This is the down season before all the tourists and Ayson's friends from his other life come stay.

"Ah, so we lucked out." Enya raises her eyebrows.

River nods, "We sure did girl." She likes Enya. There's a fire within her.

"He's a wonderful man Enya."

"Oh…Ayson? Yes, he's been so welcoming and the work he's done on the Logan's house is-"

River smiles sweetly, "No I mean he's truly an incredible person honey. You can rest easy with it. Ayson is a hero in this town. You'd never know as he rarely talks about it, or…himself. He actually saved the Logan's. Both Beth and Edgar were dying after being hit head on two minutes from leaving this house. They won't let him pay rent and insists he live here as long as he wants."

"Oh my." Enya had no idea.

"Yes, he ended up here in Hixon after his wife and daughter drowned in the ocean at a birthday party back home. He left there and never really goes back."

Enya frowns, "Oh how awful."

"He ended up here and we so *love* him. He belongs in Hixon. He's healing from *his* past but he heals so many here just by *being* around. There isn't anyone in Hixon that doesn't know Ayson Ford."

"I can understand that."

River grabs her hands, "I'm not sure why I'm telling you all this. I know he looks rough around the edges. The long hair and the tattoos but, he's got a heart of gold." River chuckles.

Enya smiles not sure of whats happening but she knows she likes hearing him spoken of so highly. River appears to her as winding and fluid as her name. She widens her eyes and leans in whispering to Enya, "Hey, you wouldn't by chance enjoy getting high would you?"

"Who me? Well of course..." Enya smiles.

River claps her hands, "Hot damn. I knew I like you girl. Where's my bag."

"Oh, there's some in my bag right there behind you." Enya points.

"You are full of surprises!" River grabs the bag and hands it to Enya.

Passing a yellow and red blown-glass pipe between them they joke about men who cheat and the good women they lose because of their cowardice. Ayson and Frank return with more beer and some chocolate covered strawberries. Frank nudges Ayson and whispers about how his wife is a handful if she takes more than two puffs.

Enya leans away giggling and interlaces her fingers with River's whispering how free she feels now that her husband-baggage is gone. She looks over and sees Ayson watching her. He's smiling from ear to ear, admiring her tossed hair and dress hiked up above her knees. She furrows her eyebrows and picks up the pipe in offering. Ayson hands the beer to Frank and moves over to sit behind Enya on her blanket. He opens his legs placing them on either side of her and when he leans forward to take the pipe from River, she feels the heat of his chest against her bare back. The smells his musky scent mixed with laundry detergent swirl all around her and smell heavenly compared to the staunch skunk scent of the pot. His touch sends waves of desire coursing through her suddenly, which she brushes off as the high.

Frank places the items down between them and follows Ayson by sitting behind his wife waiting for his turn with the pipe.

"My, my ladies, we were in the kitchen slaving over melted chocolate on the stove for *your* strawberries and here we find you've started dessert without us."

Ayson's voice reverberates velvety behind Enya's ear raising all the hairs on the back of her neck. She instantly wants to feel his lips trail kisses along her back and feels her sex begin to moisten.

Enya sees the plate of strawberries, "Oh my gosh, River look at what they did."

River, already hazy-eyed looks over, "Ohhhhhhhhhhhhhhh gentleman, you can prepare our strawberries anytime! These look maaaarvelous."

Enya cracks up laughing at River her infectious guffaw sending both Ayson and Frank into hysterics. Frank grabs his girlfriend's shoulders lovingly.

"I think it might be time to take this party home honey what do you say?" His eyebrows wave seductively.

River saddens, "Oh did I go to far Frankie?"

Ayson laughs knowing Frank has other ideas in mind.

Enya stands abruptly, "I...need a dick, I mean a dip...in the pool!"

All of them crack up laughing. Enya points towards the ocean and begins walking. River starts to stand to follow her, "Me too En, me to-"

"No, nooooo honey. You can only do that if you can swim remember?" Frank yanks on her skirt.

Ayson realizes Enya is half-way to the ocean and that she didn't have the greatest time earlier in the day. He follows hoping to persuade her to come back to the fire.

Frank yells to Ayson, "Hey man, we're gonna take off and let you two enjoy the rest of your evening. See you Tuesday?"

"For sure guys. Hey, drive safe."

River turns to her man kissing him, "Those two are done my love. Completely *smitten*, they just don't know it yet."

5

WOULD YOU

"Kiss...me."

Enya continues towards the waves illuminated only by the moon and the fire Ayson started. She laughs to herself thinking about the fire he started within her just a few moment ago by sitting behind her and letting his chest hairs tickle the soft skin of her back. She pulls at the sides of her dress lifting it up and over her head, letting it fall to the sand while still walking towards the quiet of the waves. Next her underwear comes down and onto her finger which delightfully flings, heaving them up and over. Ayson catches them and lays them on her dress continuing after her. *How high is she?*

"Oops!"

"Uh-" He's not quite sure what to say. The voluptuous shape of exposed body distracts him in the best ways.

Enya laughs uncontrollably completely forgetting she's stark ass naked next to the adonis of a man she met only that morning. He laughs looking forward not sure what to say...trying not to stare. She continues to step toward the waves the water actually warmer than the air.

"Are you absolutely sure you want to do that Enya?" He turns to her, his smooth voice non-judgmental.

She stops wondering why he asked, then she remembers he saw her earlier in the afternoon struggling in the waves.

"Oh right, well I don't have to fight my bikini to stay on now do I?" She flips her hair back looking at him over her shoulder.

Ayson thinks she's got a magical beauty, rare and stifled. Her ass is perfection and he feels desire for her that he knows isn't from the pot. He grapples with the thought of if he should go in or not. He doesn't want to leave her. She steps on something and her knees buckle a bit. He steps forward to catch her, the heat of her hand unraveling him somewhat. The water reaches mid thigh and the waves are cresting right at her mound which he can see each time she turns around to smile at him. He loves her little feminine landing strip of golden-red hair that matches the long strands that hand down her back resting at the crest of her behind. His cock hitches in his bathing suit. This is a different Enya from the stressed out version he met early this morning. He can see that she's wild inside just waiting for someone to allow her to be herself. Enya turns quickly running and before he can think, he's trotting in after her. He knows there's no going back now.

Ayson reaches her as she stops abruptly turning around. He grabs a hold of her wrapping his arms around her as she begins to fall, too far in to withstand the force of the waves. Her nakedness pressed against him causes arousal, the feel of her breath against his neck making him want to taste her. Enya wraps her arms around his neck looking into his eyes, loving all she sees.

"Kiss me."

"What?"

"Kiss…*me*."

He looks at her long. She's been waiting and he understands he no longer has to. He's wanted to taste her since she climbed out of her Jeep.

"I-"

She tilts her head, a sadness washing over her. She lowers from her tip toes, her breasts retreating down his chest. He's losing her. He grabs her face with his hands looking deep into her eyes, he knows he wants her. He looks from her lips to her eyes, and then her whole face wiping her hair out of the way. He looks at her lips part and leans in. There's no going back now.

Ayson presses his lips to hers, an eager hunger yet he holds back. Suddenly she parts them, their tongues uniting and slowly intertwining feeling like velvet together. He exhales, relaxing and deepening, feeling her body press into his, her arms come around and up under his arms to his back. She spreads her fingers wide and splays her palms across his back feeling sculpted muscle between her fingers. Tasting him causes her warm fluid to move from where it began, preparing her just a bit more. Her womb begins to pulse and ache, wanting him inside her...filling her. He smells so good, she moans into their kiss causing him relent to his growing erection. He brings his arms down and around her body, feeling her softness, holding her protective and tight to him. He begins growing harder and she likes it. She presses her hips forward to let him know how much she likes his body. A wave comes in pretty hard forcing both of them to step sideways. He grabs her tightly from falling but breaks the kiss.

She looks up at him knowing she shouldn't even ask but she's so tired of never getting to say what she wants. Her sister told her it's time for a change.

"Ayson, I know we just met and all but I'm gonna…"

He smiles, waiting.

"Well, I'm just going to come out and say it. Would you? Uh- I mean…"

He bends to look into her eyes, "Would I what Enya?"

She looks from him over to the fire and the tent. River and Frank have left, they're alone. She looks back at him.

"Would you…take me to your tent?"

6

BLISS

"I want you."

Ayson kisses her deeper, cupping her jaw with his free hand. He's propped up on the other elbow, her body cradled to his side. They're laying on the memory foam pad in his beach tent. He's never had a woman in his tent with him. It's nice. The opening in the top shows the moons luminesce in and onto their skin causing a elegant silhouette to make love to. The sounds of the ocean waves crashing in the distance create an ambiance of cozy protection yet while still in nature. She likes his hidden space.

Enya moves her hand up under his long curls pulling him closer and then into her mouth. She wants him. The feel of his chest against hers creates a thrumming between her legs with warm fluid preparing and lubricating her most sacred area. He is an exquisite kisser! Patient, slow, sultry, and gentle. He's un-rushed as if he's creating art. His tongue, soft and relaxed, ignites all her senses and she yearns for him to enter her physically but also within her psyche. He has an intense energy. She really likes him.

Ayson releases from their kiss to look at her. He's trying to reconcile how he only met her in the morning but feels as if he's known her for a lifetime. Using the back of his fingers he steadily caresses down her cheek, her neck, and then to her wanting breast. Her nipple erect and fevered, aches for his play. She likes how he uses touch to communicate. He lowers down moving his mouth over her mound exhaling and blowing a cool breath causing a bounty of sensations. He kisses the sides of her rotund flesh then teases the skin down her rib cage and up again to circle and suckle her plump, wanting pink aureola. Enya feels all her nerves ignite and send arousal throughout her body, instinctively she arches up and towards his mouth wanting more of his oral indulgence. He's exploring how she responds and what her erogenous zones are. So far she's astonishing, creating his deep desire for full connection. Continuing gradually to her second breast he gives equal attention but this time takes her nipple between his teeth and holds it a moment to assess her breathing. Enya moans long then exhales, cupping his cheek and pulling his teeth into her. She likes his timing and that he cares about being tender yet hungry.

Spreading her hand from his face to his chest and then down to his rippled stomach, she continues on to find the drawstring to his bathing suit, still wet between them. She kisses the top of his head while he stimulates both her now begging, fevered nipples. He's now grabbing her full breast and bringing it to his mouth tracing his tongue along the nipple edges. He sucks hard for only a second then releases sending a shock wave within her causing her yoni to respond the same. Enya clenches her legs together to feel the pleasure of her swollen vulva against her clitoris. *Oh he's very good.*

Her hand opens the front of his suit and she slides her palm down finding his long, turgid thick shaft. Spreading her fingers wide she gently encloses his sex within her grasp, loving how smooth his skin is in contrast to his rigidness. She pumps lovingly, just enough to cause him to groan reverberating her breast still in his mouth. She squeezes his girth again...and leisurely *again*, enjoying the vibrations his deep voice sends through her each time he moans. He loves her touch. Enya smiles a moment with the thought running through her mind of how just this morning life seemed so dismal and now here she is being swallowed up by this absolutely gorgeous man who is enjoying her. She really, REALLY likes him. He has a slow, yet assertive nature and a passion for perfecting everything he sets his attention on. He likes giving her attention.

Enya slides her hand from him around to his behind trying to remove the only item of clothing preventing their union. She wants to feel him in her. Ayson releases from her breast and helps her free him, pushing his suit down his legs, kicking it across the tent out of their way. He feels freed of the mesh lining, enjoying her decision. The coolness of the air feels liberating yet can't distract from the deeper desire and yearning to enter her slick heat. Before he can return to touching her dreamy curves she unexpectedly slides down his frame. She clutches sweetly around his large girth again and pulls him fully into her hot, wanting mouth. The feel of her enclosing around him causes a deep moan to escape. Ayson sucks air through his teeth moving his hands up to hold his head. Every nerve below his waist ignited as he succumbs to her succulent oral diversion. She takes him deeper into her throat and he can hardly stand the madness as every fiber of his body begins firing off in reaction to her sultry tongue. *She's so fucking good.*

Enya suckles leisurely but rhythmically, he's almost afraid to breathe for fear of erupting. He feels as if she has complete control. His lungs hitch and he struggles to inhale. She brings a second hand around his upper shaft and begins moving both in opposing directions effortlessly, creating deep sensations while swirling her tongue on his swollen head. He feels as if he might die and yet he's already feeling as if in heaven…

Enya tastes a drop of his precum and likes how warm and slick it is. He tastes healthy and the shape and texture of his cock is remarkable to her. She especially likes how erect and sizable he is against her snug mouth. She moves a hand down his shaft and softly cups his scrotum massaging and caressing his testicles. She's enjoying the perfection of his body and wants to explore even more of him.

Using her tongue she trails steadily from his head down one side of his shaft, licking and gently dragging plump lips down until she reaches his sack with her lips. Placing tender kisses on his warm skin, she pushes his leg open wide to lean in farther and take one testicles into her mouth. Enya softens as she suckles, tugging tenderly so as not to hurt him. Ayson sucks air into his body again unable to believe the pleasure she's invoking. He feels as if he may lose his mind. No woman has ever been so detail oriented with his most sensitive areas. She moves to the second testis giving it equal attention as he did with *her* breasts.

Ayson cranes his head forward to see her mouth on him in the glow of the moonlight. She's an alluringly, passionate lover with exquisite oral technique. He thinks her husband an imbecile for discarding her so unsympathetically. He decides it's time to show her how desirable she is but, she suckles more and he has to lay his head back again against the pillow to keep his composure.

Instinctively he brings a hand down to cradle her head and takes a handful of her silky hair as she continues to please him driving him to near lunacy. He opens his sleepy eyes to gaze up at the moon giving silent praise to the universe for her. Her rapture then takes all words and language from him.

Enya begins gradually gliding up his shaft, peppering kisses and tongue play up and over his end.

The feeling sends surges of nerve pleasure through out his entire body. He doesn't know if he's ever been so aroused. Her hand comes up to find his chest she grabs one pec between her palm, squeezing and massaging, feeling his own erect nipple, pressing it between two fingers. She releases her mouth from his sex and climbs up his large frame to place her hot mouth onto his ready nipple. Suckling with flicks of her tongue she hears his deep moaning again. *He's so easy to please.*

Ayson slides his hand tenderly down between her legs finding her soft hair and swollen mound wanting his grasp. Enya likes how he touches her and squeezes him. Carefully he massages her folds and her surrounding vulva. He loves the feel of her lips and crevices silken along his fingers. She's piqued with want for him and he yearns to taste her. First he slides two fingers long and deep into her tight opening, her head flies back releasing his nipple and a gasp escapes her while she squeezes around his fingers. She releases and squeezes tighter. Enya is excited to feel him deep inside.

"You...*are so*...ready-"

She nods and agrees, "I want you." She's so happy she met him. She needs his connection and his pleasure is more than she could have imagined.

He slides in and out super slow, taunting her womb. Her warm fluid escapes lubricating his palm more. He reaches in farther gliding in then out...in then out...a few more times until her breathing hastens, he must taste her. He turns her and slides down the bed taking her into his mouth before she can even fathom whats happening! He brings his hands around to her tush and pulls her onto his face as he lays on his back. He buries his mouth into her sacred yoni, gently sucking and tugging at her hooded clit. Enya cries out into the tent at the sheer pleasure he invokes and can hardly hold onto the sheets, feeling as if she's falling from the earth and heading towards heaven. He moves a palm along her perfect rump, gliding in towards her cleft and pulls her cheek open. She moans and as he suspected she enjoys anal pleasure. *She's incredible!*

He caresses his fingers down her opening from behind and uses her slickness to lubricate up and around her skin respectfully preparing her. His mouth continues to suckle from the front, her taste and warmth remarkable. His fingers from behind encircle and burrow lovingly waiting for her to release and allow entry. Enya can't take the pleasure any more and as he enters her sweetly from behind and suckles her clitoris from the front she lets go and begins crashing into surges of bliss convulsing and shuddering beneath his tongue. Her head flies up and Enya wails beautifully and long into the night.

Ayson loves how she comes and lets her pulse and pump over and over until her head lowers to the sheets and she's breathless...spent. Just the sounds of her made him want to explode. He grants her patience and a moment to enjoy her orgasmic afterglow. He moves his mouth to the side knowing she'll be sensitive and suckles at the inside of her thigh. Slowly he releases his fingers from her backside, letting her rest and enjoy the pleasureous result of their intimacy.

Enya decides she doesn't need much rest and lifts up to moves down his huge frame until her lips find his. She kisses him longingly and rewardingly. No man has ever pleasured her so completely. *He is amazing*. She wants him!

Ayson cradles her to him enjoying the feel of his erection against her soft stomach skin. She feels so good on top of his body. The weight of her, the scent of her, the shear delectation of her energy ignites him.

Suddenly, she breaks their kiss and moves up and glides her fluids up along his shaft, moving her folds and warm lubrication slowly up…and down him. *He's so…big!*

Enya mounts him, putting him at her opening. Slowly, without a word she gazes down at him and sinks inch by inch down on top of him opening to his gloriously, massive size. Her tightness engulfs him fully and he buries snugly deep inside her womb. Ayson lets out a gasp grasping at her waist! The feeling near mind-blowing!

Enya smiles down at him knowing she's enticed him the way he did to her just moments ago. It's been so long since she's wanted to please a man. He's perfect and deserving of her yoni energy. She can't believe the snug size of him against her firm walls. He thrusts his hips up tenderly and buries himself deeper feeling how incredibly tight she is around him! Enya clenches him and begins a slow rocking to massage along the bulk of him tantalizing his every nerve ending. She sinks down deeper onto him and squeezes him with each new thrust and pulse he gives. Ayson moans and sucks air in between his teeth again. The quiet sounds of his pleasure in the tent arouse her. She can feel he's so close and waiting for her again. He's an amazing lover and she thinks about how much she likes *him* inside her most sacred space. He moves and spreads her open making her feel like her vulnerability is needed by him and that she's safe. She knows this isn't often felt with a lover. Ayson is different.

Enya spreads her hands along his broad chest pressing him into the sheets then eases up to sink deeper again. He stares up at her as if she's the most beautiful creature he's ever seen, a goddess. She loves his dreamy, seductive eyes. She loves that they crossed paths and for a moment thinks she wished she'd met him years ago. She feels Ayson is the type of man a woman *wants* to be bonded to...the type that makes a woman want to succumb to his rapture!

Leaning down she finds his mouth and kisses him deeply while moving rhythmically along his divine cock. He grasps the back of her head and juts his tongue hungrily into her mouth while thrusting his hips up and pulling her ass in reaching up into her deeper. His movements become more hungry as he gets closer to climaxing. He's enjoyed her slow torturous tantra. It's brought them both to a point of no return.

Releasing her plump behind he knows he's getting close. He brings his hand around with his palm flat along her mound and his thumb downward finding the hood to her swollen clit. He sweetly presses and circles his thumb while thrusting up deep into her! Enya sucks his tongue as he's setting a faster, more desperate pace. He massages her clit just a bit faster in rhythm to his hip thrusts, and a little faster. She moans into his mouth and tries to retract but he holds her head snug to him, kissing her more, ensuring she'll cum along with him! He want to possess her climax.

Ayson thrusts and releases, then thrusts and releases again, feeling surges of intense energy exchange between them. Her nostril breathing becomes erratic and he knows she's beginning to crash over threshold, he begins to let himself go, his own release and hot fluid starts to pump and he feels her squeeze as if she's pulling his soul from him. Enya moans long into his mouth and he joins her as both of their bodies convulse at the same time, pumping and loving together. She grasps his hair clenching down around him never wanting the ripples of pleasure to stop coursing through her. He spills into her deep, pumping and throbbing. Pulsing...and pulsing...

The waves of ecstasy begin to relax them, their bodies releasing their holds, long and languid breaths beginning to slow. Enya goes limp on top of his body, heaving breaths along his neck. He lets his arms fall to his sides. Both of them gasping for air, clinging to each other...

7

MORNING AFTER

"my weird"

Seagulls squawk intrusively while flying by the tent window. The sunlight peaks through illuminating their cozy tent. Enya inhales a deep breath stretching her legs out as Ayson smiles then kisses her.

"What are they complaining about out there?" Enya whispers to him.

"Oh the sky rats? Probably nothing. They don't know it's Saturday and the world is supposed to sleep in."

She runs her hand through his hair admiring it's length and beauty, "It is Saturday isn't it? Oh yay…"

He moves his hand down her shoulder to her hip, "Yay? Sounds like you're looking forward to another day here in Hixon."

"I sure am." She kisses his lips loving how warm and sleepy he is upon waking.

"I'm certainly looking forward to it now that you're here." He presses into her lips gently with his. His body presses next.

"That's really kind of you to say."

Ayson smiles, he means it. He is enjoying her company, her connection, *her everything*... He doesn't know much about her but he knows he likes her energy and that they have amazing sexual chemistry.

"It's true. I was just going to drown myself in home repairs until my shift on Tuesday but, if you're going to stay..."

"I *am* and maybe even until Tuesday!" She smiles and gives a little shrug.

He chortles liking her morning mood, "I'd like that. Hey, I don't even know what you do! There's so much about you I want to learn."

"Okay, what can I share?"

"Hmmm...well, I am curious as to where you uh learned some of those magnificent skills you showed me last night."

Enya throws her head back and giggles, "You think I have skills? I think *youuuuu* have the skills mister paramedic."

"That's different. Purely platonic life saving stuff."

"Oh, I definitely see how you can save lives." She flatters him.

He giggles deep, "You're a lot of fun you know that?"

"Uh, my sister calls it "my weird" not so much *fun*."

Ayson leans in and kisses her again tenderly. She's so beautiful. He likes that she doesn't seem to care about that or fuss. She accepts his kiss and deepens it by sharing her soft, heated tongue. He already awoke hard, but she's creating a familiar ache. He pulls away not sure if he's imposing.

She smiles watching his lips, she likes kissing him. "Hey, where'd you go with my good morning kisses?"

"Did you want to grab some breakfast in the house...or use the bathroom?" Ayson juts a thumb over his shoulder trying to be considerate of her needs.

"Not really, I think I'd like to have breakfast with you right here if that's all right."

He sees a fire in her eyes and knows what she wants. He has no problem meeting her request and rolls over on top of her spreading her legs open. She kisses him and takes him into her wanting body again…

8

DEVOUR

"I loved every minute."

"I write for Rolling Stone actually."

Ayson's eyebrows raise, he had no idea she was a writer. "Holy shit really?"

"Really." Enya eats the last of the bagel he toasted and buttered for her as she swings her legs sitting on the counter watching him make tofu scramble. She looks up and down his gorgeous body, a towel wrapped tightly around his small waist, muscles bulging from everywhere else. She realizes he eats very well and keeps in shape. It looks good on him, self-loving. He's very good for her.

"I had no idea. I actually pegged you for maybe a yoga teacher or…"

Enya giggles.

"What, was I totally off?"

"No, I love yoga. I think it keeps me sane. I also enjoy weightlifting here and there too."

Ayson furrows his brow and smiles gorgeously. He doesn't say anything.

She pushes his arm, "What?"

"Nothing. I mean I can see you've got a rockin' bod there Ms. Writer but that ocean seemed to spank you yesterday in the balance department." He teases her.

She laughs throwing her head back, "Okay yes, I was not able to display my balancing techniques yesterday, I'll admit that but, I was way too distracted by losing my bathing suit bottoms to look anything close to composed."

He likes how she formulates sentences and even more that she can laugh at herself. Many sensitive women like Enya can tend to draw inward when teased. His paramedic humor can often offend...but she's different.

"The bikini was amazing on you but it seemed a bit too big? I vote for the evening attire."

"Evening attir- ohhhhhh you mean when I just threw my dress on the sand and went into the ocean stark naked?"

He smirks, "The dress aaaaaand your underwear ended up in the sand…and I'm not complaining at all."

"I was a little high. River and I started way earlier than you and Frank." She giggles.

"I loved every minute." He turns the burner off and throws the spatula to the side. Walking to her he forces her legs open and leans up to kiss her. Remembering all they'd done and how much fun she is, he wants her *again*. She ignites a hunger in him.

Enya feels his hands come around and grab her behind from the counter. She likes him…A LOT. He has a libido much like hers. He parts her lips exploring her sweet taste with his gentle, loving tongue. She wraps her arms around his neck feeling him press his hip into her while pulling her body to him. Their fun banter has aroused him. She can feel him growing hard for her which makes her body quiver with want. She thinks about how she went from having no sex with a cheating bastard of a husband to having it more than she could have expected in the last fourteen hours.

Ayson lifts her from the counter and carries her to her bedroom as it is closer than his on the third floor. Enya moans wantonly and Ayson figures they'll eat breakfast another time, right now he has something better he wants to devour.

9

KEY

"Lead the way captain."

An hour and a half later, another three orgasms down, Enya knows she better get out of bed or she'll want to be there the whole day. She can't get enough of him.

"Okay, so how about I help you finish the porch and then we find some dinner in town, my treat!"

Ayson smiles, "I was hoping to use you as an excuse to *not* have to paint today. I don't mind building a porch but painting it is not my favorite part. Besides, I think we should rest no?"

"Oh, did you need a break from it?"

He turns towards her wiping a strand of hair away from her eye, "I think so. I can finish it tomorrow. I'd much rather take you on an adventure…and then for that dinner in town, but *MY* treat."

He kisses her nose, looking into her eyes completely enamored with what she just did to his body. Admittedly, he needs to give his body time to acclimate to all the extra curricular activities as its been a *very* long time since he allowed himself to be so free.

"An adventure? I'd love that. What did you have in mind?"

"How do you feel about boats?"

Enya likes his adventurous side, "I love boats. I'll just have to get a better bathing suit so I don't end up going overboard!" She laughs feeling childishly excited.

He chortles, his deep voice echoing in her large room.

"I won't let that happen. I can't fix your dangerously unsafe bathing suit."

"Aw." She rewards him with a kiss. "I like the way you fix things.

He smiles at her, his large frame shaking the bed as he exits it. He walks gorgeous and naked over to a desk on the far wall of the room and opens the top drawer. He finds what he's looking for and closes the drawer holding up a pack of unopened safety pins. His boyish grin brightens the room.

Forty-five minutes later Enya steps onto Ayson's fifty-five foot Azimut Express Cruiser he has docked at the Hixon Marina ten minutes from the beach house. The boat is stunning and suits him. Not really fit for a party but perfect for a couple. She's impressed that he owns a boat.

"Ayson this is beautiful!"

He's pleased, "Thank you. It's my little escape vessel. Not too much to take care of, an excellent way to decompress after a long shift."

"I love it. It's so…you."

He laughs holding both their bags and walking towards the steps going down into the galley.

"Would you like a quick tour or need to use the bathroom?"

She nods, "Lead the way captain."

Ayson disappears below and she follows. The boat is decorated beautifully in a contemporary motif. Enya feels is quite sexy.

The steps spill into a tiny kitchen and living room area with a u-shaped couch. The colors are navy and creams with a shiny teakwood color cabinetry. She walks a few steps farther and sees a breathtakingly adorned bedroom with built-in drawers, tv, and bathroom. She especially likes the large round bed that's exquisitely dressed with throw pillows and fur blankets. It's ruggedly masculine and reminds her of his bedroom at the house. He's a very clean person. Another attribute she's impressed with.

"Oh my...I like this..." Her eyes follow the clean lines of the room and she looks like a child exploring in nature.

"I'm happy you do, did you bring a change of clothes by chance?"

"I did...as you'd suggested." She looks up at him and lingers, visions of his hands on her body while she on his bed.

"Great. We can stay the night if you want or head back to the house later. It's up to you."

Enya can tell by his overnight bag he'd prefer to stay, she obliges, "I think I'd love to stay and experience how you escape in such a enchanting space."

Ayson is pleased and rewards her with a kiss. "I like your writer-words."

"Oh you do? Well, I have way too many stuck up in this crazy brain of mine so anytime you want to hear some…"

"I don't think your brain is crazy at all and I very much enjoy your…what does your sister call it? Your *weird*?"

"That she does."

"Well, I especially like your weird…although it seems much more refreshingly normal than weird."

She wraps her arms up around his neck and kisses him again.

"Thank you."

His crotch hitches and he feels a want for her again. He's surprised at how aroused just the sound of her happiness makes him wild for her. He pats her bottom, the feel of her beneath his hands creates a hunger he tries to push away.

"I'm going to go get everything ready for us to head out to Reiner. There's a store here at the marina, I'll grab some food and wine we can enjoy and cook out on sandbar. It's a great place to barbecue and swim if you're up to it."

She nods, "I am so up for it. I'm gonna use your restroom and then I can run to the store and get what you need."

"That'd be great Enya." He smiles not wanting to let her out of his arms.

Enya unloads all the items, Ayson had on his list, onto the counter smiling at the old man behind the register. His name tag says **Saul** and he looks as if he was born and raised in the marina store. She wishes she had brought her purse to pay for everything but Ayson insists the owner puts it on his tab.

"Find everything ya need ma'am?"

Saul's voice is hushed despite his rough exterior. He appears overly tanned and sun-worn from the sea. Enya smiles admiring the "Cracked Ass Saloon" T-shirt he has on.

"You wouldn't happen to have skewer sticks would you?"

"Naw. Ayson has them in the top right kitchen drawer though."

Enya looks up into his light blue eyes realizing old Saul knows Ayson very well.

"Oh uh, okay."

"New around here huh?"

"Yes. My first time."

"Nice to see him with such a beautiful woman if ya don't mind my sayin', that is one good egg there that man." Saul points a crooked finger out the window towards the Saviour.

She smiles sweetly, "I think so."

"Got my heart going after I fall dead on the dock over there." Saul points out the window in the opposite directions towards where the gas pumps are for filling up the boats.

"I thank god every day that boy was washing his boat just a few feet away."

Her eyebrows raise, "Oh my, I'm glad he was!"

"Never seen him with anyone before. You may be the first since he moved here years ago. All the ladies want him round' here. Ya'll headed to Reiner?"

"Uh, Reiner?"

"Reiner is a favorite sandbar of Ayson's. He and his crew eat and camp out there most weekends. They keep me in business."

She smiles, "Oh well then I believe so. He mentioned we were heading to one of his favorite places."

"Yeah that's Reiner. Don't be surprised if a whole bunch of them emergency people show up for the weekend. Firemen, cops, even the coast guard guys love to party with Ayson. He's kind of a hero around these parts...and not just because he got my ticker going. There's a lot of folk that owe that man their lives. Not just the tourists neither, I'm talking natives from the area. He's a stranger that wandered our way and became family real quick."

Enya looks over and sees Ayson moving about on the yacht preparing things. She admires that others think of him so highly. She feels proud to be able to spend time with him. Her ex never had anyone say one damn nice thing about him. She thought he was kind and others were jealous of him. That's what he would tell her anyway. She learned the hard way to listen carefully to how others speak of a man you date. If they say nothing at all, that's *saying* something. Trent was a terrible husband and an even worse friend. Enya feels good about Ayson. This time she's going with her gut instead of being coerced.

"I love hearing that."

"Okay, let me get you rung up and stop chewing your ear before the big guy comes looking for you."

The door chimes indicating someone entered. Enya cranes her neck wondering if it's Ayson. Her heart jolts and her stomach feels sick when she recognizes his scowl. There, standing behind her in line is her ex, his arms crossed over his chest the way he does when he interrogates and bullies her. She pivots, fear begins coursing through her veins.

"What do you want?"

Saul hears the firmness in her question. He looks out the window hoping Ayson looks over.

Trent Ryan stares down at her, his face stoic, anger seeping from his body.

"Where's the lock key to the combo handle on the safe?"

"I have no idea. I don't touch your shit."

Enya turns her back and puts her hands around the box Saul packed up for her. He looks her deep in the eyes to see if she's in trouble. She gives him a side smile embarrassed at having to deal with her unfaithful spouse.

Saul looks over her head, "Can I help you sir?"

Trent raises up a six pack of beer he grabbed from the shelf as he walked up to her. "Just this."

Saul hands Enya the box without moving his eyes from the fat stranger. The man looks as if he'd been driving all night.

"Ma'am, tell Ayson this is on his tab. You have yourself a good day now."

Saul gives her a reassuring smile. His deep tan wrinkles showing slight white lines.

"Enya!" Trent raises his voice to her.

Enya turns, "How many times did you harass my sister before she told you where to find me?" She hates the way he hounds her only sibling. Jenna would never reveal her whereabouts. He must have threatened her husband.

"I didn't bother your sister."

"Oh, so now you're what tracking my car?" She's fuming at how he must have used his car salesmen abilities and contacts to find her. He's a man of little talent but surely knows how to use others to get what he wants.

Douchebag.

Trent steps around her to place the beer on the counter and pulls out cash. She doesn't like his movements or how close he stepped. She tries to step around him. He moves in.

"I need my key En, I know you have it so why don't you just hand it over and I'll be on my way."

Enya knows thats not true at all. If his mouth is moving he's lying. She knows she doesn't have his key. He knows she doesn't have it either. She's alarmed that he's come so far for a key he knows she doesn't have and one that he has a copy of.

One of your stupid sexual conquests probably robbed you stupid.

The door chimes and Saul nods his chin. Enya sees Ayson standing just inside. He came looking for her. She takes the box and tries to get away from Trent, her stomach feeling sick and her fight-or-flight response kicking in. She knows Trent is a coward and only bullies her when there isn't an audience. She doesn't want Ayson involved in the drama and something that's completely beneath him. Trent is not worth it.

"I told you. I don't have your key. I have no need for it or for any of your possessions. Leave me alone."

She rushes towards the door meeting Ayson halfway, "Hey you, I'm sorry I took so long."

"Everything all right?" He sees she's upset, he looks over her to where Saul and Trent are at the counter.

She smiles nervously, "I'm ready to go."

Saul gives Ayson a look as he turns to follow her out. He can sense Enya's energy and looks back again at the chubby guy at the counter looking back at them. He sizes the guy up and wonders if he somehow harassed or offended Enya. She's a stunning red-headed beauty and he can see how men could take that as an in to make inappropriate comments.

Enya walks hurriedly to the yacht. She tries to push away her adrenaline and the triggers invading her mind. Trent is the last person she wanted to see on such a beautiful day. Her eyes affix on the beautiful navy cursive font that says "Saviour" on the back of the boat. She climbs aboard and turns back with a smile for Ayson. He's watching her, carrying the box. He glances one last time towards the windows of Saul's store. Trent is still at the counter. He wonders if he should leave her and round back to the store.

Saul raises a hand and waves. Ayson nods then boards.

She exhales trying to relax.

"Enya?"

"Yep."

"Are you all right?"

"I am. How long does it take to get to your tiny island?" She takes the box from him and turns to step down below to the kitchen. Ayson watches her, frowning.

"Oh it's about twenty-five minutes north of here. I'm ready if you are." He wants to comfort her but senses she needs a moment. She'll share when she's ready.

Looking back at Saul he sees him wink and knows he's talking the fat guy's ear off so they can leave. He takes the signal and walks to the controls to get them out of the marina.

10

STALKING

"I actually like your distractions Enya."

As they make it out to sea passed the buoys, Enya finds him and wraps her arms around his broad chest from behind. He clasps her hands with one of his and steers the boat with the other. She reaches up on tip toes kissing the back of his ear. He's a very tall, large man. *In all the right areas.* She like it! He can feel her hands trembling. He cuts the engine and turns around to give her the moment she needs. He learned a woman needs attention and contact when *they* need it, not when a man feels like giving it.

She looks different. A fear in her eyes. He's seen it so many times before with trying to help accident victims or those on the gurney in the ambulance. Pure fear.

"Enya, I can help. I know we don't know each other all that well yet but, I can help. It's what I know. I see fear in your eyes sweetie." He speaks softly, yet a serious tone.

She tries to fake a smile, "I came here to escape a situation for the weekend. I just wanted to forget about it. Give my body and mind a rest. You know?"

"I can understand that but whatever it is has robbed you of peace in the last half hour. Give me a shot. Sometimes just hearing yourself say the words out loud can help the mind reconcile what it's dealing with. Trauma is a funny thing."

She knows he knows trauma. She knows he's right. She relents, "The guy back there in the store?"

"The stocky one?"

"He's fat." She nods.

"Okay?" Ayson half smiles.

Enya cracks up laughing at his expression, he's trying to be nice. He laughs in response, loving how she deals with the truth.

"He's my soon-to-be ex-husband and I drove an hour and a half to get away from the town he's in and the fucker comes here to accuse me of taking a key of all things."

Ayson frowns, "This guy stalking you Enya?"

"What? Well…I don't know. He wouldn't say how he found me. I mean, at first I thought he may have harassed my sister to tell him. But she's not like that. She hates Trent. She wouldn't tell. So I figured he tracked my Jeep or maybe my phone? He may have pressured my sister's husband." She squints confused.

"Okay. Are you…afraid of him?"

She shrugs, "Well I wasn't. I guess…well, I don't know. He cheated. I left. Two years ago in fact. I've been alone. Like I told you, I found him recently in bed with another of his victims and he should have been at work. I decided to take a weekend away, after some convincing from my sister and her paying the Logans for the room, so here I am. I mean he got what he wanted. The bachelor life, blaming me for everything, he even got two years with no pressure from me. Now, it's time for the divorce and here he is."

"Sounds like he didn't get what he really wants. Maybe that's why he's shown up. Have you ever threatened him or… indicated reconciliation?" Ayson tilts his head searching her eyes.

"Maybe. I don't think so. It doesn't matter. He knows I don't care anymore. I think because I stopped reacting it's scaring him. I mean I caught him in the act and basically just grabbed my files and walked out.

He was running after me and saying things like "what did you expect" and I just said *nothing*. I have no love for him as a person. It's gone. And, I don't have his stupid safe key so-"

"Has he ever done this before or is it new behavior? Shown up randomly, I mean." Ayson is concerned for her safety.

She looks up and to the left indicating truth, "Uh yes, it's sort of something he does, shows up uninvited or randomly. He used to do it when I worked for others. Just would appear in my office or be sitting in a chair when I returned from a meeting. It was weird. "

"Okay, has he ever seen you with another man?"
"Nope."

Ayson nods, "Huh." He bites the inside of his lip taking note. In his experience men who cheat are often sociopathic narcissists, they think they have the right to do what they want but their spouse should not have the same freedoms. He could be a problem. He decides he's going to talk with Chief Braden about this, just in case.

"I'm sorry Ayson. I know this is-"
"What's he do for a living?"

"What oh, uh Trent sells Mercedes cars, er…he's a financial manager rather." She looks unenthused. It's not something she was proud of for him.

"And you write for Rolling Stone Magazine?"

"Yes. And…well, I have a few published novels." She points in the air. "A sixth almost finished."

Ayson is impressed, "You're an author? And work for the magazine?"

"Yeah. But not *this* weekend." She smiles and steps toward him not wanting to discuss her asshole husband or career anymore. She hugs him and he reciprocates beginning to understand her ways of avoidance. He feels bad for her. She's so wounded by a man who can't see how lovely she is. She slides her hand from his back down his waist to his tush and caresses him. He feels the familiar stirring within.

He kisses her head, "Hey now, if you start that we'll never get out to Reiner."

He understands her passion now and why she's so good at pleasure. She's desperate to heal every time this guy psychologically abuses her or tries to knock her off balance. He has no problem with her need for a creative outlet.

"That's true. Okay, how can I help?"

"With the boat or…"

Enya cracks up laughing at his humor, "With getting us to your destination. I don't want to be more of a distraction today."

Ayson turns around to start the engine, "I actually like your distractions Enya."

She smiles snuggling into him as he cradles her under his arm. She's really enjoying their easy connection and the sex has been incredible! She exhales and decides he's way more worth her thoughts than Trent. She vows to push it away.

"Can I help with the food below?"

"Nope. Stay right here and keep me company, that's all the help I want."

She giggles, "I can do that."

11

HUMBLE

"You make me smile."

Enya opens her eyes and sees him standing over her unknowingly creating a seductive shadow above her. The sun feels so good on her skin. The smell of his sunblock, the breeze, his stunning physique…it all feels so good. She's fully relaxed again. Her stomach growls as the smell of his cooking mixes with the ocean air. He saves lives AND cooks, she thinks how Ayson is damn near perfect.

"Hey sleepy head. I know I told you to go take a nap while I cook but no fair looking so scrumptious, distracting me from the food. You ready for some nourishment?"

She yawns then smiles seductively, "I love your nourishment."

He smiles from ear to ear not saying a word. He bends to offer her a hand, happy his safety pins helped her overly large bikini fit for the afternoon so far. He wouldn't mind if it fell off either.

"Is that a dimple I see?" She teases.

"Come on you."

"It is a dimple! Look at that, did I make you smile?"

He pulls her to her feet, her long hair falling from the messy bun she had it in. She looks exquisite. He pulls her in close whispering.

"You did. You make me smile a lot."

"Good. You make me smile as well."

She kisses him tenderly, appreciating how sweetly he woke her. He wraps his arm around her waist and picks her up kissing her deeper. A song changes on the radio. Bob Marley begins signing a happy tune. He slides his palm around hers and begins swaying to the song, cradling her in in his embrace. She likes how he can make everything feel good.

Ayson looks down into her eyes, his green eye color is mesmerizing, his gaze piercing into her. She feels her chest beating, he ignites something deep in her.

"I like how your body feels against mine Enya."

"I really like that too."

"And how your lips feel against mine."

"Hmmmm…." Enya moans.

"I especially like how slow we can be, it *feels*…"

She waits but he just stares at her not needing to find words. He stops talking and leans in, his lips pressing intensely with hers. She tilts her head to deepen the connection, opening to him and sliding her tongue in to taste him. Ayson grasps her neck under her ear and secures her. He wants her to feel safe in his hold. Her tongue glides soft and slow. She's getting him aroused *again* with her oral play. She drives him wild.

"I think we should visit your pretty bedroom for a moment." Enya points towards the "Saviour". It's anchored just a ways away in the beautiful ocean waters of Hixon Island, South Carolina. Ayson looks towards the boat and considers her request. The food will be just as good cold. He takes her by the waist and steps to get them both to the boat.

"Well hey now! Look at you two." An older man, tall with a cooler walks up behind them. He's got three women following.

Ayson turns realizing Chief Braden had docked his boat on the other side and walked over with his wife

Treana and her two sisters who tend to fight for Ayson's attention.

"Oh hey, there's the man." Ayson offers his free hand and keeps Enya in the other. He introduces her to them and more friends arrive. They must have gotten wind of Ayson's whereabouts. Plans for their bedroom play will have to wait.

Enya sits up in a low beach chair swirling her feet in the sand. She likes the feel of it between her toes. Lunch feels amazing in her stomach. She'd been overly hungry from all their sexual energy. Ayson is a wonderful cook!

Looking up, she watches Ayson and his friends jumping and heaving for the volleyball. She smiles seeing how competitive they are and yet so respectful to each other. It's nice to see the teamwork and hear all the innuendos and jokes. That was never possible with Trent. He was the guy that made sure everyone didn't want to show up. Ayson seems to be the *reason* so many want to be together. She even heard one on their phone say, "Yeah, Ford is here."

A few more arrived and joined. She admires him. She looks around at all the differing ages and wonders how many of them he saved...not unlike how he's saving her. Oddly, she feels as if she's known him for much longer than two days. He seems to affect others with his pleasant infectious energy. Enya places her hand on her heart, it's beating faster. He does something to her.

Ayson dives for a ball and saves it sending it over the net just in time, he doesn't fall and instead catches himself dusting some sand from his hands. One of the ladies gives him a high five. He's looks over and sees her watching. His smiles widens somehow for her. Enya loves how his face brightens and his white teeth show upon smiling. He's a stunningly beautiful man and more so because he doesn't seem to care. His skin glistens in the sun, the lotion enhancing every strategically placed tattoo. He appears to have quite a story written on his body and she smiles holding a hand up to wave, thinking how she wants to know more about that story. She hopes to get to know him in a way that he'll want to share.

Next he heaves his large body up and spikes the volley ball just missing the net ending the game. Everyone cheers on his side and they all slap and hug.

Enya loves seeing them all celebrate. Chief Braden comes towards him from under the net and they seem to walk off to the side to talk. She hopes everything is okay at work.

12

TAGS

"I don't want to see her hurt."

"So what's up bud?" Chief Jeffrey Braden pats Ayson on the back.

"I'm not sure if it's anything but I just wanted to mention a strange incident that happened earlier... maybe get your take on it." Ayson hands him a beer from the cooler near their feet.

"Sure."

Jeffrey Braden is a large, slender man of Irish decent. He's known for being a team player and really good boss to his employees building a strong family sense within Hixon amongst law enforcement, fire personnel, and first responders. His wife, Treana, is a nurse. She's over sitting with a few other nurses she works with and had met Enya but wasn't overly warm.

Ayson steps closer, "So as I was prepping the boat to come to Reiner this morning, I looked up and saw this big dude watching the marina from a uh, black Nissan Pathfinder but with dealer plates."

"Uh huh." Chief Braden sips his beer squinting from the sun.

"So I see him, a big guy about five nine, two forty watching my girl go into the store."

"Aw no, Enya right? She's really something."

"Yeah, turns out this guy is her asshole ex-husband, Trent Ryan, some Mercedes car salesmen. Well, soon-to-be ex.. Cheated on her so she left two years ago, then just this week she goes to their home to pick up some files and catching him again in bed with a woman. She says nothing, walks out, and her sister gifts her the room at the Logan's for the weekend. She came here to get away for a few days and this guy shows up."

"Oof, she's married huh?"

"Unfortunately, but anyway when I met her she was pretty shaken up ya know, like down, just wanting to escape to Hixon."

"That's not uncommon." He nudges Ayson, smiling and referring to how they met.

"Anyway, I see him follow her into Saul's so I make my way over to the store to check on her. She's trying to get out of the store pretty urgently and want to get on the boat and away from this guy." Ayson sips his beer, concern in his eyes.

"Sure."

"So, she says he just shows up and wants his *safe key* from her. She doesn't have it, yada yada, and she wants to get away from him as fast as she can."

"Right. You want me to run his tags and keep an eye on things for the rest of the weekend? See if he's gone or hanging in the area?"

Ayson feels relief, "If you don't mind. His behavior isn't normal. I mean the guy drove all the way out here to ask her something he could have texted?"

"Yeah, yeah, I get it. It's a bit sociopathic. Listen, give me the tags and I'll call Jerry at the dispatch desk and maybe have patrol do a couple drive arounds since he really shouldn't still be here." He points his beer towards Hixon then pats Ayson on the shoulder again. "It's all right brotha, I owe ya and we need to keep an eye on things to keep our town tight right?"

Ayson smiles, "I know, I just met her man but something just feels so right about her. I don't want to see her hurt."

"Oh of course, hey you don't have to tell me man. See that woman over there?"

He moves them both in the direction of his wife Treana.

"That gal saved my damn heart. There ain't nothing I wouldn't do for her. I got you."

"Thanks Jeff. I really appreciate it. And...I hope it's nothing but just in case."

"For sure. Better safe than sorry. So what's the tag number?" He takes his cell phone out of his pocket.

"Oh and Jeff? He tracked her."

13

EXHAUSTED

"Hope to see you in the shower."

"Hey beautiful, whatcha doing?" Ayson sits down next to Enya on the beach blanket.

She's laying on her stomach reading on her phone. She looks over at him, a smile appearing. Seeing his green eyes tired from the sun makes her think of his *look* when they've been intimate. His scent reaches her and just being close makes her yearn for him inside her.

"Uh, I was editing an article my colleague sent me to look over. Hey, those were some pretty groovy moves you showed over there in that volleyball game."

"Yeah, I enjoy volleyball." He lays down next to her side looking up into her eyes.

She reaches down to kiss him. His lips are fevered and taste like coconut lotion.

"It looks like it. Great job. I enjoyed watching."

"Thank you." He likes her praise.

"Hey, so I was thinking you and I could sleep on the boat tonight...or did you want to head back."

"Naw, I think I can handle a sleepover on the water with you. This day has been fantastic, I'd like to stay out here as long as we can."

He smiles, "Well, everyone will start heading home soon. River and Frank may stay overnight in their boat on the other side but we'll be alone for the most part. Might here them partying but thats their norm."

"I like the thought of us being alone." She smiles.

"Oh, you're not tired of me yet?" He trails the back of his fingers down her spine very lightly.

She shakes her head and inhales sharply, "Nope." Looking back at her phone she silently smiles. He rests his palm on her tush, the feel of his touch moistening her between her legs.

Ayson reaches then to drag a finger down her shoulder and to the small of her back. She likes his touch and how caring he is. He lifts his head and takes his hair down. Enya's is still tied up but tiny strands of red curls have fallen all around her face. He takes his hand and encircles his finger in the spiral of a curl, his other hand tucked under his head as a pillow. He follows the curves of her cheekbone with his eyes and watches her eyes reading line by line. She blinks and he notices the length of her lashes and how he wants to kiss them.

Enya feels him staring and looks down at him laying next to her, "Whats up? I feel like I can hear your brain processing." She giggles.

He smiles, "I'm just admiring your beauty."

"Ah, you are charming Mr. Ford."

Ayson asks, "Why would he want to cheat on you Enya? I mean, I just can't wrap my head around it? You are lovely."

Enya shrugs flattered by his outward confusion, "Thank you…It's not the first time Ayson. He's just not a good guy like I thought. He cheats, blames me for it so he doesn't have to take accountability, leaves, and then he gets dumped and comes to find me for some sort of connection and forgiveness. My forgiveness button is broke. I think because I *could* love in-spite of, I got the worst of him. He doesn't love himself, there's no way anyone else will."

"Do you?"

"What? Forgive him? No, not anymore. I haven't slept with him in over two years. My love dissipated. Catching him again was just confirmation that I made the right choice by getting out of the marriage. I think, however, that he thought I'd come around. I was struggling to heal for years and he was just thinking he was giving me a timeout. Now, it seems he's desperate."

He caresses her face while listening, "I agree. I'm concerned as to why he came to find you…and *tracked you*."

"Yeah, I don't like that he found me in just one day but it is the first time I've left town and not said anything. He must have gone to my sister's house and got no answers or perhaps forced too many from my brother-in-law. It's new behavior and he doesn't like that I just left. That I could just do that. I'm sure he's not liking that I'm with you right now because he's never seen me with another man. Quite honestly, I just want him to go on with his affairs and his own life and leave me alone. My sister sent me this way to be free for the weekend. I really never expected he'd show up. I've called her but there's no reply yet. I hate bugging her with this…and you too, this drama needs to go."

Ayson nods agreeing, "It's a bit alarming. We'll keep an eye out though."

He points to his group of friends over starting up some dinner as the sun begins to set.

"Thank you. I do appreciate that…and you're friends are great. I like your world."

He pulls her face to him for another kiss, "I like *you*."

She parts his lips to taste him again, she enjoys his mouth. He so easy to be intimate with. Ayson moans slightly and breaks the kiss.

"Hey, why don't I go over there and grab us a few plates of dinner, say good evening, and meet you on the boat? Maybe we can start our sleepover now?" His eyebrows jut upwards with his suggestion.

"I like that idea a lot, I'm kinda of exhausted from all the sun exposure."

"Well then, let's do dinner in bed with a movie and get some rest." Ayson touches her nose making her smile. "I have some amazing body wash in the shower that has lavender in it. Feels really nice and relaxes the shit out of me after days like this. You're welcome to it."

Enya is flattered, "Thank you for sharing, I think I will take you up on that offer. Hope to see you in the shower."

"Oh, I'll be there." He kisses her jumps up to walk towards where all his friends are.

14

STAY

"Stay with me…"

Enya has her forehead against the shower wall. Her eyes are closed and the hot water runs down her scalp and spine feeling like heaven. Ayson steps in behind her and closes the shower door. He moves up against her, his flaccid shaft resting against the back of her tush, his hands caressing down her shoulders. She loves the way he touches her body. His energy is of a respectful, giving nature. He's the man she's always dreamt of. It makes her want to *give* to him.

He leans in and whispers, "You are alluring Enya."

Turning she looks up into his eyes. He's tan, sun worn, yet so attentive. She wraps her arms up around his neck, "You're so…"

He kisses her deeply, parting her lips and exploring her with his tongue. She feels the familiar ache he ignites deep within her yoni. Even exhausted she desires him inside her. No man has ever affected her like this.

Ayson moves his palms down her back to her waist and then slides them slowly to her plump tush, grasping her and pulling her into his growing length. He presses her clit and she groans into the kiss. He realizes she's becoming aroused in the same manner as he, she's a match for his libido and he loves it. He breaks the kiss reaching up he gets some soap from the dispenser and uses it to wash her body feeling the silky skin of her womanly physique. He loves the feel of her, white suds in contrast with her dark tan. She watches how his hands move on her body. When he gets to her breasts she moves her head back closing her eyes to feel his taunting thumb along her nipple. He's strong in his touch but gentle in how he moves. He grows harder and slides slowly between her vulva, tantalizing her most sensitive erotic zone. She can't help but pulse inside, her body wanting him. Reaching up she follows his lead and uses some soap to wash him as well. The feel of slick lather against his muscle and large size is making her heart beat faster.

"I want you Enya." Ayson's admission makes her almost weak in her knees, his voice gruff, hushed but authentic. He makes her feel so desired.

"I want you too. I feel like it's been too many hours without you inside me." Enya looks up at him. His eyes are dilated, he has a hunger that's more intense suddenly.

He moves them under the water to rinse then pushes the nozzle off. Without warning he picks her up in his arms and opens the door to walk them both to the bed. She sees the room is darkening with only the sunset illuminating through the open windows. Soaking wet he lays her down before him. Her wet skin against the breeze and clean smelling sheets is comforting. Instinctively she opens to him, her arms reaching up exhaustedly for him. He climbs forward hungrily and takes her, plunging into her readied warmth. She's so wet lubricating them both. She cries out in pleasure. He buries himself inside her begging womb, his lips crashing down onto hers. Enya moans into his mouth feeling his intensity and accepting all of him. She grabs his back hanging on, his weight pressing into her feels magical! He's so big and yet so tender and intense. He fills her and stretches her fully. He thrusts deep into her breaking their kiss to exhale.

"You feel so fucking good…" Ayson thrusts again… and again. His heart feels as it may burst in his chest but he doesn't care.

Enya can hardly find her breath, the pleasure he's sending through her every nerve makes her feel as if her eyes are rolling back. He's so good.

"Ayson…I love how you…" She loses her words as he thrusts deeper, slowly flicking her clit at the end of each long push. She feels her climax coming on strong as if she has no control. He's taking over her body and she likes it. She submits to his hunger letting him sweep over her.

He rests on his forearms holding her face between his palms. He looks into her eyes, holding her gaze as his lower body is taunting and burying himself slowly and rhythmically into her moist heat.

"Stay with me…"

She looks at him sleepily, a brow furrowing, "Stay with you?"

He nods. He wants to know she won't go. He wants her here with him…safe. He's certain of this. Even just having met her, he knows himself and what he wants. He pushes deeper watching her head lean up and back, she loves how he fucks her. Deep, intense… primal.

"Stay with me Enya."

She brings her gaze back to him. He's very serious and trying to hold on. She knows what he's asking and really has nothing to go back to. He's so much more and *everything* she knows she wants.

Ayson leans down kissing her, he retracts caressing the sides of her temples with his thumbs. His eyes are waiting, his body still teasing her below...over and over...

"I-"

He plunges further holding himself to her clit, then scooping his hips before thrusting again. Enya moans into the quiet of the room unable to control her body anymore. He's possessing her, taking her...

"I- I, think I can do tha-..."

He smiles hearing the words he's wanted since the moment she stumbled out of her Jeep and into his life. His mouth comes down hard on hers, his body speeding slightly, his movements more intense, more pleasurable pressure. She loves what he's doing to her. She can no longer hold on and desperately grabs his back digging her fingers in, wrapping her legs around him. He loves how safe she feels and carries them into freedom. They begin to quiver into their climaxing ecstasy, moving into a new level of connection... together.

15

ABANDON

"Is everything okay?"

The waves lull Enya back into a deep slumber. The feel of him holding her as her head lays on his chest soothes every worry she had.

Ayson hugs her closer then kisses the top of her head. He lays back looking at the ceiling coming to light from the sunrise.

Last night was intense. *They were intense.*

He asked her to stay after only two days. He's never done that. He shocked himself but he vowed to live life better. She's *better*.

The quiet of the room is interrupted by the purring of a boat engine in the distance. Ayson reaches up and moves the window curtains aside. He sees Chief

Braden's boat coming towards him and realizes he left his phone on the couch last night. *Shit!* He moves slowly out from under Enya trying not to wake her. She rolls to the other side and he quickly gets out of bed and tip toes out of the bedroom.

When he gets to his phone he has seven missed calls. All of them from Jeff. Now he feels bad. He asked a favor and then hasn't been available for the answer. He quickly dials, calling back hoping he hasn't pissed him off too much.

"Yo!"

"My apologies Chief. I just realized my phone was on the couch and well...I wasn't."

Jeff chuckles and Ayson hears him cut his engine, "Listen, I need permission to search the Logan's."

"Oh really."

"Yeah, we found that vehicle. It was abandoned behind Lakeland Industries. Ran the tags and it's been reported stolen bud. I made some calls and he was fired from the dealership. They couldn't discuss more. Then I found out he stole the vehicle...well, he didn't bring it back you know."

Ayson inhales deep, "Okay."

"Anyway you both can stay out here today, just in case? It'd be easier knowing she's safe with you and this guy can't reach her if he is dangerous. I need to locate him."

"Yes. We'll be fine. We have enough food and supplies for a few days."

"Good. Yeah, just to be safe we're going to take a look around the house, I'm hoping he's not hiding out waiting for her. It's not like he ran out of gas and just abandoned the car, you know?"

Ayson nods, "Right. Yeah, she says he's never driven this far but his MO is to just randomly show up at places she goes. Not sure if he's wrapped too tight upstairs."

"I hear ya. Listen, you know I got ya. We're gonna head back then. I'm gonna write it up as a verbal permission from you, the tenant. I don't think the Logan's will mind too much."

"I'll explain it to them if I have to. Maybe give them a call when we know more."

"All right brotha, and keep your damn phone near you okay?"

Ayson smiles, "Will do, Chief. I do apologize for that."

"Hey, believe me…I know all about getting distracted in the bedroom." He laughs heartily.

Ayson chortles not knowing what to say.

"I'll keep you posted."

"Thanks so much."

"Hey?"

"Yeah."

"Come up for air sometimes huh?" Chief Braden laughs and Ayson can hear him turn the engine on.

"Funny."

"Out-"

Ayson smiles hitting the end button. He looks around for his charger.

"Was that Chief Braden?" Enya is standing in the bedroom doorway leaning up against the frame in his t-shirt. She looks stunning with her hair tasseled and sleep in her eyes.

God, she's gorgeous.

His heart jumps a bit in his chest, he knows he's catching feelings. Deep feelings.

"Hey you. Yes, that was Jeff. He's actually heading back. See his boat right there?" Ayson points out the back windows so she can see the police boat heading in the opposite direction.

"Oh."

"Yeah, uh I got so distracted last night I left my phone out here and he was coming to check on us and...hey, we never ate dinner! How would you feel about homemade chicken chili for breakfast? I can heat it up."

She smiles and stumbles to the u-shaped dinette table. "I think I do need some food."

He steps to her and kisses her forehead, "Coming right up."

"So, I don't mean to pry. Is everything okay?" She knows he was talking about having food and supplies.

Ayson opens a cabinet door and clangs through some pots and pans before settling on the medium size one. She thinks he looks fabulous in his little boat kitchenette, his hair hanging down to the middle of his back and a draw string bathing suit enhancing his small waist and broad shoulders. He has a perfect v-shape to his back and an ass that flows from it perfectly!

"Yes, well I'd like to talk with you about some things actually."

"Okay." She feels a bit tense.

"So, I didn't want to worry you yesterday but I was uneasy when I saw how your ex affected you in the store before we headed out here."

"Right."

"I asked Chief Braden if he could check on that black Pathfinder he was driving. I saw it parked in the lot when I was on the boat. I grabbed the tags and Braden said he's call it in to dispatch to check it out. He also sent patrol around to ask Trent what he was doing in Hixon."

"You can do that?"

"We take care of our own here Enya. Hixon is a great place for island life with great people. Trent is a stranger."

She huffs, "I'm a stranger."

He turns and smiles, "You're *my* people sweetie. You're not a stranger."

She smiles but he can see the worry behind her eyes.

"Everyone really liked you yesterday. They've not seen me with a woman...well, one that I like."

He chuckles and she knows it's because so many try but he doesn't take the bait. Three women tried to get too close to him yesterday and quickly got the hint that he was smitten with her.

"I really enjoyed yesterday. Your uh, family is amazing."

"They are family and when I asked for a favor, the Chief jumped right on it."

She feels queasy she hopes this all goes away, "Thank you Ayson."

"Of course." He puts the chili in the pot and the flame on medium. Stirring their breakfast he turns towards her, "So the vehicle was reported stolen."

She raises her eyebrows, "What?!"

"Yeah. Braden says the SUV was reported stolen from the dealership and that Trent no longer works there."

"Holy crap."

"So, not to alarm you too much but he abandoned the vehicle behind some buildings in a little industrial park on the other side of the island."

"He's not in it!"

"No."

"Fuck-"

"Hey?"

Enya slides back against the booth looking worried. Ayson walks to her and sits next to her with his hand on her leg.

"Listen, if it's okay with you, I told Chief we'll stay out here at Reiner today so they can locate him and see what's going on okay?"

He caresses her cheek. "Just in case okay?"

"I shouldn't have come here Ayson. What if he's losing it or something? He's not a nice guy."

"Maybe he is, listen we don't know but just in case, I told them we'll be here safe. We have everything we need for a few days…I mean if you're okay with still staying with me?" He smiles remember what he'd asked her last night. He hopes they can change the subject to something more positive. He hates that she's stressing again.

"I will stay. I said I would. I mean I just need to be able to write and submit an article once a week."

He leans in to kiss her, "That's doable." He walks to the kitchen again.

"Do you think he knew what house I was staying at?" She's overthinking again.

"That's another thing Chief asked. I gave them permission to search the Logan's house in case he ditched the car and got a ride there."

She bites her thumbnail, "What if they can't find him today? Or tomorrow for that matter?"

"It's fine. They'll locate him and get him on his way. Let's not think too far ahead. Maybe he really just thought you had his safe key. Knowing Saul, he had words with him and let him know to be heading on home. Saul is like that with unsavory types. He's caught quite a few smugglers at his marina."

Enya takes a deep breath, "Oh really?"

"He's a pretty sharp guy. Gets them all on camera too."

"Oh cool! Hey, do you think he got us on video?"

"Not sure. You okay Enya?"

"Something just doesn't feel right."

"What do you mean?"

"I don't have his key...and he has a spare in the living room vase on the middle shelf. He had no reason to seek me out."

"Oh-" Ayson feels quite unsettled.

16

GRAPE

"Now what?"

Ayson walks to the front of the boat to join her. She's back in her safety-pinned bikini tanning on the boat lounger. He takes a peak at her bewitching derrière' and feels his familiar yearning. She's breathtaking despite the tension he knows she feels. He can sense it and he wants to ease all her woes. She's been quieter since breakfast.

Ayson feels on edge now knowing her ex had a spare key and still drove all the way out to Hixon to harass her. It's beginning to look more sinister than he'd hoped. He knows he isn't helping either. Her ex seeing her get on a boat with a guy couldn't have helped much. He wants to protect her because all the flags are red and pointing towards her ex wanting revenge.

"Hey gorgeous, feelin' like a beer?" He stands in her view to shade her so she can see he has one for each of them.

She smiles, "That'd be great."

He hands her one.

"Thank you. I enjoyed the chicken chili. It was amazing for breakfast."

"Yeah, that's Treana Braden, the chief's wife. She has the best recipe. I tell her I'm going to steal it from her one day. Truth be told though, I prefer when she makes a big pot of it out here and we all get to take some home. It gets better the next day as all the seasonings set in."

"Oh, well thank you for sharing yours with me." She sips her beer leaning up on her elbows.

Rubbing some lotions on his face he smiles wide, "I like sharing with you."

She giggles, "I like that too." She sees his boyish grin and knows he means more than just his food. She enjoys their playful sexual banter. Their chemistry feels very natural.

He's happy to see her smile. It makes him want her again. Something deep within makes him yearn for her more and more. He feels their connection is extraordinary and that he can help her forget the world for a while.

"So what are we going to do here on your yacht?"

"We can do whatever you desire."

"Have you ever had long stays on it or just overnights and…"

He smiles, "I used to live on this boat Enya."

"Seriously?"

"Yep. I still come and hang out for whole weeks sometimes. When I have a tough shift mostly, or when the Logan's rent the house to a group and I want to give them space."

Ayson lays back sipping his beer and crossing his legs. He feels her energy and sexual heat next to his skin. He smiles at how his body reacts to her pheromones.

She turns to face him, "What's a tough shift like? Or should I- I'm sorry, I shouldn't-"

He turns to look into her eyes, "Hey, it's okay. I don't mind. A tough shift is when we arrive too late to help someone, say a heart attack or a seizure gone wrong. Well, anything where you rush to get to the patient and there is nothing that can be done. I get a little triggered. Like a failure feeling…"

"I can understand that."

"The worst is when it's a child. It's tough on the whole crew, even if they're not on shift and hear about it later. For me, it still hurts so much because of losing my daughter and wife...being too late you know."

"River mentioned it to me, I'm so sorry Ayson." Enya reaches to touch his cheek.

He tries to smile leaning into her hand for a moment.

"I'm sure she did. It seems to go with the name, like "Oh that's Ayson Ford...he lost his wife and daughter when a drunk driver hit their car into a river in upstate New York.""

"Is that how they say it?" Enya knows she didn't hear it that way.

He shrugs, "Back home, pretty much. Here they usually just stop at "his wife and daughter died" and no one pries further. I think it's because most have a similar story as to why they landed here. Hixon seems to be full of natives and then those escaping pain. I also don't elaborate much. People can read up on it if they really dig. It's in the past." He huffs taking another sip.

"Is that why you live in the sun now?" She smiles trying to point out a positive.

He looks at her, "You're pretty sharp there hottie."

"Hottie? You think I'm a-" She points to her chest.

"Oh, I *KNOW* you're a hottie."

She reaches to tease his nipple in between her two fingers, "That's very nice of you to say."

She eases up and then very softly squeezes his nipple again, smiling and giggling.

"Watch yourself now."

He likes how she lightened the mood. He knows he'll share more. Enya is easy to talk to. She doesn't try to extract too much too soon, like others do.

Her eyebrows lift and she retracts her hand. She sits up and takes two fingers that were on her beer bottle and are now chilled and reaches again adding the chilly affect to his already hard nipple. She smiles teasingly.

"Watch myself how?"

He cants his head and stares at her. He sees she's taunting him and he likes it. Her touch gets him going. He averts his eyes down to his crotch.

She looks where he did and sees he's getting hard, his bathing suit restricting him. Her eyes widen and she smiles up at him.

"Did I do that?"

He laughs, "Ya think?"

"Now what?"

"I think you should finish that beer real quick."

Enya takes her bottle to her lips and chugs the whole thing. He watches her and follows suit but before he's done she lifts up and hikes a leg over him coming down to sit on his lap. She likes the feel of his rigidity between her yoni folds. Pressing his shoulders down towards the blanket she holds him hostage underneath her.

He laughs, "We're on the front of a boat Ms. Enya."

"Yup."

"Where your perfect ass is now in full view."

He can feel her slowly moving and tilting her pelvis into him. He wants to pull her bikini bottoms to the side and have his way with her feeling her slippery heat all around him igniting every nerve ending the way she does.

"Yup."

"And...satellites are zooming in on that perfect rocking motion you're doing."

Enya stops, her mouth dropping open and a smile forming, "Shiiiiiiiit-"

"Yeah."

He laughs out loud at her response and thinks she's incredible. Suddenly she springs upwards and runs towards the back of the boat.

"Last one down below is a rotten egg!"

Ayson likes her playful, competitive nature. He bounds down the steps and finds her backing up against the stove. He comes towards her his hands low to tickle her. She giggles hysterically bending so he can't reach her belly. He swoops in but at the last minute widens his grasp and brings her in for a hug instead of the tickle-fest she'd prepared for. She likes his embrace and reaches up to nibble his neck. Ayson's eyes close as he feels the surge of pleasure her lips give sending pulses to his already aroused cock. She drives him wild!

He reaches under her arms and picks her up, she wraps her legs around him and turns her head to suckle the other side of his neck. He tastes so good. A mixture of soap, lotion, and salt. He can feel her crotch, hot with want for him. Her nipples hard through her bikini top.

Ayson swing around to where the dinette table is and pushes the contents on the booth. He lowers her onto the table and grabs her face in his hands to bring her mouth to his. He kisses her hungrily, plunging his tongue into her sweet mouth. He breaks the kiss to pull her bikini strings and remove her top, she unties his bathing suit helping him throw it to the floor. He looks at her, his eyes filled with hunger and desire, his pupils dilated. He lowers to his knees, his face level with her pussy. Enya pulls at her bottoms and he takes them down throwing them. Ayson dives into her sacredness . His soft lips and suckling tongue fit perfectly inside her entrance. He causes her to inhale throwing her head back, her hair dangling down off the table. She grabs at his hair, running her fingers lovingly through it. The pleasure he sends through her body causes her breath to hitch. *He's so good!*

Ayson loves hearing her. He flutters the hood of her clit assessing her arousal. She's soaked already. He remembers her cold fingers on his nipple and remembers he put fresh fruit in the refrigerator. He once used a grape on someone and knows Enya is adventurous! He suckles harder and then releases.

Enya looks at him through her bedroom eyes wondering what he's doing. He holds a finger up to give her a silent signal he'll be right back. She watches him slide on the floor to the tiny boat refrigerator. He gets something and shuts the door crawling back. He looks up smiling and shows her a large grape in the front of his mouth. She smiles wildly not knowing what he's up to but liking his imagination! She trusts him because he never hurts her. He enjoys her pleasure.

Ayson lays her back on the table and comes down onto her again strategically placing the grape at the top of her opening just above the hood of her clit. The cold sends surges of pleasure through her and she gasps. He slows to make sure she likes the temperature and sensations. When she arches towards him he knows she wants it. He dives in using the little grape with his tongue to massage her rhythmically arousing her most sensitive area with a cold grape and his hot tongue. He gently slides two long fingers inside her using his other hand to reach up and grab her full breast in his palm. She moans deeply and sounds as if she may be losing control. The multiple sensations are more that she can handle and Enya suddenly arches up on the table grasping at his shoulders, her orgasm begins with ripples of pleasure she can't control and heightens to powerful spasms that make her scream out! Her body quakes and pulses around his fingers and she throws her arms up and back onto the table submitting completely to his rapture. Ayson Ford has taken her to a whole new place...on a whole new level. He smiles admiring her heaving, breathless body. He stands up watching her orgasmic bliss and slowly moves his fingers out of her. She's trembling and sensitive. He thinks she's a bewitching being of sexual energy. He wants her but he'll wait. They have all day.

Noticing how exposed and beautiful she is, he steps close and peels her from the table, picking her up in his arms to take her to the bedroom. What he has planned for them both will require space...and comfort.

17

STOIC

"What is it Ayson?"

Enya's eyes open only to slits. She sees him sleeping peacefully across the bed from her. He has his hand atop of hers. She's spent, she feels drunk but not from alcohol. He's getting more and more open and intense as the hours go on. She's loving the weekend so far. She smiles thinking she may never want to leave. Her eyes close and her breathing gets deep. Drifting off she thinks of the absolute satisfaction she feels coursing through her body from his lovemaking. He'd taken her from behind making sure to go extra slow finding her g-spot, circling and tantalizing her. The way he built up and then reached around to stimulate her clit while filling her over and over and over... His pleasure mind-blowing and beyond compare. The things he does to her body are indescribable. He's a king among men.

Enya wakes to the room in darkness. She's shocked she slept all day! The sun went down and night spread throughout the boat. She looks over but he's not there. She feels alone and grabs for a shirt to go look for him. When she tries to stand her legs are shaky. She huffs a laugh matter-of-factly. He did intensely loving things to her body and she still wants more.

Her stomach growls and she realizes she's starving. Barefooted she walks around the bed towards the glowing light in the kitchen in hopes that he's there.

Ayson is sitting at the dinette his head in his hands, his cell phone in front of him on the table. She gets an eerie feeling and slides into the booth next to him. He lifts up to see her and doesn't smile. His eyes have a glazed over look as if he wants to cry but won't. Something is not right.

Enya caresses the side of his head and ear to comfort him. If he'd smiled she would have snuggled in and kissed him but his energy is stoic and angry. She hasn't seen this in him yet. She waits.

Ayson exhales disgust and slams his hand down. She almost jolts but instead tilts her head in concern. When he doesn't speak she finally asks, "What is it Ayson?"

"Saul Gentry, the owner of the marina store?"

"Yes?"

"Chief Braden just called. Someone killed him… someone murdered Saul."

18

TERRIBLE TRAGEDY

"Just let it be what it is…a terrible tragedy."

Enya exits the interview room and Ayson stands up to greet her. He looks worn and bone-tired but not as much as she. Her eyes are swollen from tears. She's feeling stressed and a bit guilty that she may've brought horror unknowingly to the tiny island of Hixon. She answered every question she could about Trent, who is now their number one suspect for the death of Saul Gentry. A sixty-three-year-old man Ayson saved from dying. Enya feels Trent could be responsible because of proximity and timing, she just never thought him capable of murder!

The case would be pretty cut and dry if the video surveillance system wasn't ancient and damaged by whoever to took a bat to it and then took the footage. Enya was able to tell them that Trent is in fact in the fingerprinting system but the only thing she saw him touch in the marina store was a six pack of beer. She doesn't think he's smart enough to wipe his fingerprints so it's hopeful he left one behind. Nothings come of it just yet. Ayson hugs her tight for a moment and lets her breath in his embrace.

"We should head back to the boat. Officer Carda will take us."

He moves his arm around her and guides her down the hall.

Enya lays her head on him whispering, "I'm so sorry Ayson."

"Hey…you couldn't have known. Hell, I couldn't. I left Saul too. We didn't know."

He tries to help her feel better. It isn't known if Trent Ryan actually killed Saul by blunt force trauma but it's looking as if he had and he's nowhere to be found.

Enya gave them all she could about her ex and even allowed them a few photos off her phone. She wishes she could do more. As much as she's falling for Ayson, she wonders if she shouldn't have come to

Hixon. If it weren't for her, probably none of this would have transpired.

Enya hands Ayson a hot cup of tea. He sets his phone down and moves over so she can sit with him on the bed. It's the middle of the night and neither of them can sleep. The boat is rocking a bit more than usual and she's not sure if her stomach is protesting the waves or all the interview questions.

"Anything?" She looks at his phone.

He puts his arm around her, "Not much. The scene is still being processed but Saul's been transported to the morgue. They'll finish at the store soon and close it up. Every officer is out combing the island. There's only three-thousand people here and only so many places to hide so…"

"Yeah."

"Braden and his detectives are on it. He wants us to stay here until further notice. He didn't like having to bring you in but they had to video your interview."

Enya shakes her head, "I just hope it can help. This is just awful Ayson. I'm sure this sort of thing doesn't happen here."

"Well babe, murder happens everywhere, especially on islands."

She turns to look at him, "Listen, I want you to know that this has been probably the best weekend of my life up until well...all this. I want to thank you. And...I'm sorry Ayson. I am so sorry if my life and past brought this here. I had no idea-"

He cuts her off, "Hey, hey, hey...listen to me, as much as I'm pissed about Saul, I need you to know I don't blame you. I'm not him. I won't put everything on you like your ex. You did nothing wrong by wanting to come here. I want you to know I don't regret meeting you or anything we've shared."

"Uh-"

"No listen, I know your knee-jerk reaction is to blame yourself and try to little this down to you making a decision to come here and how none of this would have happened if you hadn't. That's trauma sweetie. That's what the mind does. You're trying to reason in an unreasonable tragedy that you had no control over. I've seen this before with many of my employees, hell I've done it myself, it doesn't help to abuse yourself in an uncontrollable incident. It's like everything is so out of hand guilt is the only controllable thing. You don't have to "do" anything. Just let it be what it is…a terrible tragedy."

Enya sees his eyes water. His words ache within her, she knows he's right. He's so beautiful.

"Thank you." Her voice hitches and she can't speak, a tear rolls down her face. He places the tea on the shelf and pulls her into his chest.

"Let's try to rest."

"Yeah."

No more words are needed. He feels his body react to the weight of her on him. She feels an ache, a sadness even, deep inside and she wants him. He heals her with just his touch.

Hours later the morning sun begins to light up the bedroom, she can't help but begin to wake. A lump has formed in her throat and she feels as if she's pushed her tears down and mixed it with the fear. She reaches out for him, he cups her hand instinctively. Somehow she moved far away from him. She lifts her head and he's staring at her. The intense look in his eyes is something she hasn't seen yet. She moves in and he reaches to touch her face. Enya stops to cover his hand

and closes her eyes at how tender he is. He caresses her cheek with his thumb. When she opens her eyes she can see his pain, a immeasurable pain. He stares with no smile. She knows he's gone to a place of darkness, perhaps he's remembering the loss of his family. She stares into his eyes, fear washing over her that he's caving. She knows if she pries he'll go deeper. She says nothing.

Enya reaches her hand and mimics his touch on his cheek. A tear forms but he continues to stare into her. She feels he's slipping deeper. As she caresses him he blinks slows, his tear trickles down and she stops her thumb to catch it on his cheek. His pain is radiating out from some gaping place, he must lock up. She doesn't want him to feel he has to do this. She wants to let him be the man he is around her. He should feel his emotions and not have to push them away. Vulnerability is not weakness…it's strength! She takes a chance and leans in. Laying close she places her forehead to his. He inhales and then exhales a sigh twice as long. He holds her gaze. She senses he needs her, she wants him to need her…to know it's okay.

Taking the chance she presses her lips sweetly to his, no movement, just touch. Ayson allows it, he likes the feeling.

Enya needs him, she wants him. With all thats going on she still wants *him*. Not to forget or push everything away…more because he heals her, and she him. She thinks how sex used to be for a need or her ex's self-serving gratification. Not now, Ayson isn't a taker. She wants to feel him, she needs him but she's not sure what to do.

She presses her lips again, a little further. He kisses her back his breath exiting slowly through his nose. She opens her lips just slightly and gently curls her tongue within his. The feel of her attention and sweetness sends a surge of arousal through him. His sadness pushed aside he meets her with his own tongue. She opens to him letting him know everything is all right. He deepens the kiss pulling her neck with his hand, reaching into her warm mouth. She's so accepting. He needs her!

Ayson reaches out and she moves into his embrace grasping him with her body, lulling him with her heat. He's unsure, she's not. Enya spreads her hands along his back and pulls him into her heart. She rolls him onto his back and mounts him sweetly and slow, he doesn't have to think. She breaks the kiss to ease down onto him, welcoming him into her healing womb, cradling him, protecting him, loving him even during sadness...

Enya makes loves to him to the slow rhythm of the ocean waves taking away all that is wrong. She's been on the other side of loneliness in the dark times, she wants to heal him as he's been healing her. She looks into his eyes, no words spoken, pulling him into her possession. She leans down spreading her fingers into his, holding his arms against the bed, his heart open and exposed. He stares into her eyes submitting, allowing her to take him to a place he's hidden for fear of hurting again. He succumbs to her, letting her guide them to a new kind of freedom.

19

NOT MOVING

"Stop!"

Enya shuts off the shower water and grabs a towel. Bringing it to her hair she dries off wondering why Ayson didn't join her as he said. He may have fallen back to sleep.

The boat shakes and a loud noise comes from the kitchen. Fear courses through her.

Did he fall?

She flings the door open and runs wrapping the towel around her. Calls out, "Ayson! You okay?"

The clang of dishes and pots hit the floor. Something is not right! Enya leaps out of the tiny bathroom, passed the bed, and out of the bedroom.

Trents body flies past her hitting the windows above the booth and crashing down onto the table.

Enya screams out of shear fright. Ayson steps towards him, his eyes glazed over in rage. Trent falls from the table, gets to his feet and charges Ayson, a sneer of rage erupting from his round body. The two collide Ayson going for Trent's neck, Trent heaving punches at Ayson's stomach!

"Stop!" Enya screams at her ex. Ayson throws his head towards the opposite wall of her, causing him to stumble and lose balance. Ayson doesn't want Trent going near her.

Trent catches himself then pushes off the wall and jumps towards Ayson again.

Enya runs to the sink, there's a knife and a cast iron pan. She takes both losing her towel on the floor. Turning she sees them attacking each other again.

Ayson catches Trent preventing him from using his weight to take him down. Trent outweighs him but Ayson has the strength. He cuts in low around Ayson's waist backing him up and smashing him against the counter. They smash into the cabinets shaking the boat again. Enya sees Ayson shift his head to the side with Trent in a bear hug and takes the opportunity to heave forward attacking Trent from behind. She can't let him hurt Ayson!

Trent goes down slow...his body falling to the floor lifeless.

He's not moving.

20

MAYDAY

"Enya! Enya, call for help!"

She stares down at him, her nakedness fully exposed. A knife in her left hand, the pan in her right. Ayson falls to Trent's side assessing his pupils, and feeling his carotid artery. His chest is heaving from the adrenaline and fight, Enya's too. Ayson jumps over Trent's body and bounds up the steps to retrieve his emergency bag from the top deck cabinets. He jumps back down and kneels aside of Trent. Opening the bag he begins pulling out medical items and a neck collar.

Enya is standing frozen looking down at them, then to each of her hands. She drops the pan on the floor causing a loud thud. Trent does not move. She looks at her left hand and throws the knife at the sink. She can't believe she just killed him. She's never hurt another human in her life!

Ayson looks up at her. In a calm, even voice he says her name. She sees his lips moving but there's pounding in her head like a heartbeat.

"Enya?"

She's standing frozen...naked.

"Enya...*Enya*...**Enya**...."

She's looking at his mouth, then down to Trent, then back at his mouth moving. He's opening things and moving quickly, his eyes are back on her.

"Enya?"

Her hands tremble, he sees she's going into shock. He needs her not to be a second victim. He reaches to clasp her wrist. His touch warm and soft, "Enyaaaa?"

Her eyes avert to him, she can hear his beautiful deep voice. She can hear her name come from his lips. Her eyes lift to his, she can hear him!

"Enya? LISTEN TO ME. Go put clothes on. I need your help honey. Can you Help me?"

She can hear him! "Ye-" She nods.

"Good. I need you to call for help. Enya? Can you do that for me? Can you call for help?"

She nods and steps to the towel. She picks it up and puts it around her. She looks back at Trent. Ayson is trying to help him after he was just trying to kill him! His large bloodied body lays sprawled out on the floor, his eyes closed, mouth open.

"Enya! Enya, call for help! I need you to go up on deck and call for help. Say mayday, mayday, mayday and tell them the Savior needs 911 for an unresponsive white male with a pulse. Head injury! Chief Braden will get them out here! Enya go!"

She turns towards the steps with her towel on and does as he instructs feeling as if she's not in her body. Things are blurry, she sees her hands moving, sees the receiver, she turns the button on and picks up the CB. Her voice is hushed, she pushes words out, none legible, she tries to breathe and speak again. The CB crackles and clicks when she pushes the button it gets quiet so she tries again.

"Mayday-"

She lets go of the button, more static, she pushes the button and brings the receiver to her lips, "Mayday, may…Saviour…please, I killed him…"

21

LOVE VS BANE

"I- want you too."

The phone vibrates against the hotel nightstand. Enya shuts the light off in the bathroom and walks to it, sitting on the edge of the bed. It's Jenna. She knew she'd call again before she has to leave. Her sister always calls at the right times.

"Hey." Enya tries to sound present.

"I just wanted to check on you one more time."

Enya blinks, smiling slightly on her end of the phone.

"Thanks Jen, I'm dressed and ready."

"Tough day sister."

"I don't want to do this."

"I know. I don't want you to have to. I didn't want you to have to go through any of this. I'm so sorry if sending you away for that weekend messed everything up En. I just wanted you to have some peace."

Enya nods, "I know, I know. Ayson was the peace... Trent the war." She tries to huff a laugh.

"I am sorry Enya."

"Stop Jen, you weren't the reason all this happened. I just wish I'd never met Trent. Everything would be fine if I'd never met him...never married him."

Jenna feels for her sister, it breaks her heart how much she's had to go through with this guy.

"Well, how could you know..."

"Yeah-."

"Anyway, I'll be there when you come out. Just because Trent had no family doesn't mean you don't. I love you En."

"I love you too."

Enya rolls the suitcase to the door and turns to take a look at the hotel room she's lived in since that horrible night. It's been weeks. She can't say she's sad to see it for the last time. She'd much prefer to have stayed with Ayson at the Logan's but, with the damage Trent did to their home looking for her, and the boat still a trauma trigger, it was best that they stayed away. Truth be told, she only sleeps now when Ayson is beside her.

Looking down at the dashboard of the Jeep she thinks of how she'll be happy to be rid of it soon. The road to the hospital is one she's memorized over the last few weeks. The tall grasses along the sides wave in the wind, the beach sand peeking out from the dunes. This will be the last time she'll drive this road with the weight of the world on her shoulders. The guilt is still fresh, the trauma intense, but no more will she have to drive towards it.

The phone rings through the dash, it's Ayson. He's calling to check on her like Jenna. She blinks slow, gratitude for those who love her and check in.

"I'm on my way." She speaks softly, the feeling of a lump lodged in her throat.

He's relieved she answered, "I'm sorry I'm not with you En. I'm still wrapping up this shift."

"It' fine babe, I think I need to do this alone anyway…like we discussed."

"I'll be there as soon as I can."

"It's just a bunch of legal paperwork…and then the waiting."

He calms his voice, "It's much more than that baby."

Enya knows how he feels about not being able to save Trent. Despite doing his best efforts, the hit to Trent's skull was too critical. His brain injury is on *her* hands. She's the one that has to deal with it. Technically she's still his wife.

"It's a burden I have to carry Ayson. I don't want you going over all the things you think you could have done differently. It happened. He came unhinged with how his life went. He tied up River and Frank on their boat, watched us on yours until early that morning, he attacked you, you were trying to protect me, I was trying to protect you, I reacted…you tried to save him…"

Her voice cracks and tears burn the back of her throat. She hates how everything went down. She hates that she brought this to such a lovely little island like Hixon, to *his* world.

"Enya, it's still self defense no matter how you try to take on the blame. You saved my life. Everyone knows it. We can't save his. It's not meant to be."

She huffs trying not to breakdown. She remembers watching him trying to save Trent on the floor in the boat's galley. She wants to feel good about what he's saying. She wants to admire that she saved the love of her life from the bane of her life. She wants to be okay with using a cast-iron pan against Trent, instead of a knife. She wants to believe Trent laying in a hospital bed brain dead is better than him going to prison for attempting or actually to murdering them. There are so many things she wants right now but knows the only remedy for all this…is time.

"I am happy for *your* life Ayson."

"I love you Enya Ryan. In one weekend, one tragic, trauma-laden weekend…I fell for you. I never knew so much could happen so quickly but when I think about the other side of it all, I see all the good you are. I want that. I want *you*."

Enya veers to the side of the road and puts the Jeep in park. His words take her breath away. She's wanted to hear what he's saying her whole life. Because it's coming from him, because he's so true, it means the world.

"I- want you too. I've always wanted you. All that you are…I-"

He hears her without even needing her words.

"You're going to get through this today baby. You're stronger than any woman I know. And once you do, once you get done with that terrible moment, I'll be the one waiting on the other side of the door for you. In fact, we'll all be there for you. You're new family… here in Hixon. You belong here Enya. You belong here…with us, with me. You always have."

ABOUT THE AUTHOR

Dezi Golden is an American author and former tantric life coach residing in Las Cruces, New Mexico.

www.ingramcontent.com/pod-product-compliance
Lightning Source LLC
Chambersburg PA
CBHW051948170626
46808CB00007B/2529